ESCAPING MADNESS

ESCAPING MADNESS

LIVE FREE OR DIE BOOK THREE

HAYLEY LAWSON

MICHAEL ANDERLE

ESCAPING MADNESS TEAM

Thanks to the JIT Readers

Mary Morris
John Ashmore
Paul Westman
Micky Cocker

If we've missed anyone, please let us know!

Editor
Lynne Stiegler

To my family, thank you for your on-going support.

—Hayley

To Family, Friends and
Those Who Love
To Read.
May We All Enjoy Grace
To Live The Life We Are
Called.

—Michael

Ryder didn't know if she could kill Afana and rescue everyone held hostage in the bunker, especially since it looked like Leandro was going to be Fluffy from now on. What she *did* know was that she and her friends were going to try.

Ryder watched Fluffy as he ran ahead toward Massimo's home. His white tail was wagging, and he looked happy. She hoped he was. Ryder recalled the conversation she'd had with him about being a wolf while he was still Leandro. Leandro had said that he loved the feeling of being free when he ran. Perhaps that was why he was running now?

That thought warmed Ryder's heart. Maybe the reason Fluffy couldn't turn back to Leandro was that he was now in his true form, as a wild thing. She had mixed feelings about that. She missed Leandro but was also glad that Fluffy was back. Either would be good when they got to the bunker, but Ryder had a feeling Fluffy would be more ruthless than Leandro, and *that* was what they needed. Fluffy would rip Afana in two.

At least she hoped he would.

Ryder was flagging by the time they approached Massimo's. The fight with Sergei and Yegor had sapped every last bit of her energy. She trailed behind the others, every step a monumental effort since all she wanted to do was curl up in a ball right where she was and take the longest nap in history.

Well, at least I'm not taking a dirt nap like those two assholes. She smiled and winced at the sharp pain in her cheek. She knew there'd be a nasty bruise there tomorrow.

Carter slowed down to walk beside Ryder. "Penny for your thoughts." He was still wearing the sweater Tightwad had given him. There were little flecks of glitter in it that caught the fading sunlight; he looked like a fairy had sprayed the glitter on him. She smiled, then winced a little when the movement caused the already-tight skin under her eye to stretch.

Ryder grinned at Carter. "I'm thinking you look like a colorful muppet."

Carter laughed. "You're a fine one to talk. Have you looked at yourself?" He sniffed and waved a hand in front of his nose. "Or *smelled* yourself, even?"

"I was in a fight!" Ryder protested. She took a whiff of her armpit and cringed a little.

Carter wasn't going to go easy on Ryder just because she'd been in an epic battle. "What, with a horse?"

Ryder looked down at her clothes and noticed they were, in fact, covered in a thick layer of stinking muck. That had escaped her. "Those fuckers. They must have dragged me through manure. If they weren't already dead, I would rip their heads off and stick them up each other's asses."

Carter laughed in response. "Who smells now?"

Payback is a bitch! He's loving this after I got him to wipe shit on his face when he was at the mountain settlement cleaning the toilet areas. Difference is, I'm not scared of a bit of shit.

Ryder gave him a snarky look and quickly brushed two globs of muck off her clothing. *Time for a bit of fun* "Come here, Carter. Let me share..." Ryder moved toward him with her dirty hands raised.

Carter ran like a Mad was after him. Ryder laughed despite her aching bones and chased him, waving her hands at him. He looked over his shoulder. "Fuck off, Ryder. I'm going to be sick!" he gagged for effect, then almost for real.

Ryder was used to the smell from having grown up with horses. Funny how shit smelled familiar to her and reminded her of happier times.

She stopped chasing Carter when he disappeared into Massimo's house. Chasing him inside with shitty hands would have been more than a little disrespectful to the vampire who had opened up his home to her.

Ryder ran a finger over the scarred arm of the wooden chair on the porch, the one she'd carved her knife into the armrest of on the night she found out the truth about Leandro and Massimo. Well, they hadn't really been lying. It had been more an omission, and mostly on Leandro's part since he'd been too afraid to tell her the truth in the first place.

She'd have to see if she could fix it if there were time.

Her first priority was rescuing Terrier and the others from the bunker, then she'd fix the chair. She turned to follow the others into the house and crashed nose-first into Carter's back. Carter was standing behind Massimo, who was frozen in the doorway. Why were they hanging around?

Ryder leaned past Carter to see what was happening.

It was a fucking mess.

The house was eerily quiet, but Fluffy wasn't growling, so Ryder didn't think there were any Mad inside. From the state of the inside of the house, it had been trashed. Massimo's stuff was everywhere. They had left the place spotless. Leandro and Carter had cleaned off the blood splatters from the Mad Ryder had killed. Massimo's precious books and records were scattered on the table, there was a pile of plates with leftover food on them, and chicken bones and beer bottles were lying around everywhere. It looked like someone had been partying while they were away.

First Massimo's bar was trashed, and now this, Ryder thought angrily. She heard the fridge door close and peered into the kitchen to find Massimo with a beer to his lips.

Massimo took a gulp and looked at all of them "How rude of me. Come in. Would you like a beer?"

Ryder was a little shocked at how calm he was. *I nearly killed someone in the bunker for stealing my blanket.* She caught herself mid-thought. *Oh, wait, I did kill him.* Yegor was the one who had stolen it.

Massimo shrugged. "It's just stuff. We've checked the house, and the testicle professors are gone," he told them straight-faced. "It was the scrotum biscuits Ryder took care of."

Ryder cracked up, laughing so hard she began to cry because of all the bruises on her ribs. "Massimo, you're killing me!"

The vampire cracked up as well. "I've been trying to work that into a sentence all day!" Massimo admitted through his tears.

Massimo waved everyone into the kitchen. "Come on, everyone. Let's have a drink to the fallen and our victory." He spread his hands wide and made a small bow. "Kelvin, drinks are on the house."

Kelvin grinned and got to work as if they were in the Old Dog. "What would you all like to drink? You can have anything you want, as long as it's beer…"

Kelvin passed Ryder and Tightwad a glass of water each. After today, that was exactly what Ryder needed. Since she was with friends, she could loosen up a bit. It might also help with the pain.

Massimo took a beer from the fridge and poured it into a dish for Fluffy. Ryder recalled that Massimo had said that Leandro didn't drink much as a person, but maybe he was a little more relaxed as a wolf.

He headed toward the dish.

Massimo raised his beer, and everyone followed. Well, except for Fluffy, because he had no hands to raise his glass. "To good health and new friends! Today we won the battle, and tomorrow we will win the war!"

Afana glared down through the glass floor of Level Five at the traitor, Terrier.

He slammed his fists on the glass floor of Level Five, so fixated on his desire to break through and get to Terrier that he didn't register that the only things being damaged by his repeated blows were his hands.

Afana hissed and snarled with rage. He wanted Terrier's heart in his hands, and he would have it. His skin split, and blood splashed on the glass floor with every punch. He knew it wouldn't break since he'd had it made from of unbreakable glass. *This whole goddamn place was unbreakable!*

A Mad ran toward Afana, and he swiped his hand sideways and knocked the Mad away like he was no heavier than a leaf.

It didn't matter how strong Afana was. He couldn't get through the glass floor.

"No!" Afana screamed in frustration. More Mad came at him, and he smashed them out of the way too.

The Madness had overtaken the bunker, and Afana's search for Terrier was going too fucking slowly because of it.

That bastard had stirred up this revolt inside the bunker, and now he had the gall to stand there and look Afana in the eye. Afana looked up through the glass to Level One, where the advisors were at their computers.

He fixed Terrier with a chilling glare. Let the cattle believe it had hope. Soon he would override the door to Level Six, and kill Terrier slowly and painfully. Afana needed to get back up there and override the system. This was *his* bunker, he controlled it, and no one was going to lock him out of his home. *No one.*

He bared his fangs at Terrier and screamed through the glass, "I'm coming for you, motherfucker. Enjoy what time you have left before I tear you to pieces."

Terrier couldn't hear what Afana was screaming because the levels were soundproof, but Terrier didn't need to hear the words to get Afana's message. He wanted to kill Terrier, and everyone on Level Six was in danger now because of him.

Ryder, hurry up!

Afana pounded on the floor, then swatted the Mad like they were flies. *He's going to rip me in two.* Terrier wasn't easy to scare, but he was shitting himself—and with good reason. Afana was a badass and completely crazy vampire who was out for Terrier's blood.

Afana got to his feet, his shadow falling over the terrified people on Level Six below. He screamed at them again and jumped up through the hole in the ceiling, then gripped the glass around his drop hole and pulled himself up.

"It's okay," Terrier told the people around him. "George has locked the door to this level. Afana can't get in here."

Everyone on Level Six watched as the vampire crawled all the way up the glass to Level One. Terrier was glad he'd left, but he knew the vampire had gone to work out how to open the door to Level Six.

Terrier turned to Advisor George. "George, can anyone on Level One override the doors?" George didn't answer;

his eyes were locked on the drop shaft. Terrier looked at Murray for assistance.

General Murray gave Advisor George a gentle nudge. "George? Answer Terrier."

George noticed that Murray was talking to him, and he shook his head and frowned. "What?" He looked blankly from Murray to Terrier, who repeated his question.

George paused again until Murray prompted him. "Yes, they can override the doors," he told them.

Everyone listening in on the conversation had an *"oh fuck"* moment. They'd thought that when George had locked the door to Level Six and the drop hole they were safe, but Afana was on Level One now, and he was going to work out how to open the door.

They were screwed.

2

Massimo was having somewhat of an open house. The group all spread out to relax, from the kitchen to the porch.

Fluffy was walking between everyone like he was trying to work out where to sit, or that was what Ryder had thought until she spotted him with his dish in his mouth. He dropped it in front of different people's feet and they in turn poured some beer into his dish.

The sneaky fucker was getting drunk! Massimo would be proud of him.

Carter headed over to Ryder. "Hey, smelly, I got you a drink." Carter passed Ryder a glass of water.

"Are you trying to get me drunk?"

"Of course," Carter replied with a grin.

Ryder took it anyway, since it would help ease her pain...or maybe it just took her mind away from the pain. Either way, it worked.

She smiled at Carter and clinked her glass to his. "Cheers."

Carter winked and took a seat on the sofa. "You're welcome."

Ryder dropped down next to Carter and sighed. She was at the limit of her energy. She'd had a shower; it was the first thing Ryder had done once she'd finished her glass of water and no longer smelt like horse shit. She remembered teasing Carter about her shitty hands and laughed.

While she'd been in the shower everyone had helped Massimo get his stuff put back, so the place was looking back to normal. That made Ryder feel better. She hated that Massimo's house had been trashed by Sergei and Yegor because they were looking for her. *I'll apologize to Massimo later,* Ryder promised herself.

Massimo wasn't upset about it at all. He had his favorite ABBA tunes blasting from the record player so the people inside and outside could hear them. Ryder could also hear Massimo giving everyone a blow by blow account of what had happened, even though everyone had been there. He was good at telling stories, leaving out the horrible scary parts and embellishing the heroic parts.

Ryder smiled fondly. *The kids in the bunker will love him.*

Carter looked behind him at the group and then at Ryder, "We've got a good team. Do you think it will be enough to beat Afana?"

Ryder looked at everyone. They were chatting away about the fight. Carter had a point. They were good, but were they good *enough*? Including Ryder, there were ten of them. Could they really take over a whole bunker? "I hope so," Ryder admitted. "I have to believe we are enough.

Besides, we also have everyone in the bunker who wants to escape," she added on a positive note.

Carter wanted to get into the bunker just as much as Ryder because he now knew that his little sister Natalie was in there. He frowned at Ryder, the movement almost causing his eyes to disappear under his shaggy eyebrows. "I've never seen Afana or the generals," he admitted. "When they took Natalie, I was at the watering hole at the far side of our settlement where we wash our clothes. What I did see was the destruction they left in their wake, which was enough to show me their power." Carter's happy-go-lucky demeanor dropped away. He was clearly in a dark place when it came to his sister's fate.

Ryder had seen him go there before. *Time to pull him out of it*, thought Ryder. "Afana doesn't leave the bunker. He's a different type of vampire than Massimo. He can't go out in the sunlight. But he's bigger and stronger than ten men. I'm not sure if he's smarter than us, but I know he doesn't have the heart and determination that we do," Ryder said warmly. "Now drink up, you wussy. You're looking like a lightweight." She clinked his glass again and downed half her drink.

Carter laughed and shook his head. "Me, a lightweight? *You're* the one drinking water."

Ryder raised her eyebrow and smirked. "I can switch to alcohol if you'd like? Of course, it will be embarrassing when I totally drink you under the table." She liked the idea.

"You know, that's just cheating," Carter complained. "Have you always been able to get drunk on water?"

Ryder nodded. "Yep. Well, as long as I can remember.

The first time was funny. My mom thought I'd stolen my dad's alcohol and tore him several new assholes. Then one hot summer's day soon after, I drank loads of water, and it clicked for my mom. After that, I was on cow's milk. No water for me." Ryder sighed happily; she remembered the day as if it were yesterday. She shrugged and took another sip. "We're living in a world with vampires and were-wolves, and now the Mad. Is it really so crazy that water is like alcohol to me?"

Carter grinned. "Can't a guy be jealous? It would be way cheaper to get drunk on water."

"True," Ryder agreed.

The two were quiet for a moment as they remembered their lives before Afana. They looked at one another after they'd finished their drinks and smiled.

Ryder wondered what he looked like under his wild hair. She could see that the warmth had returned to his brown eyes. She'd cheered him up and gotten him a little merry at the same time, and it sounded like the other men were getting merry as well. They were Massimo's merry men.

"Hey, are you guys having a party without me? And I've brought all the toys."

Ryder turned to see Graham. The blacksmith did look like he had some good toys. Ryder and Carter glanced at one another and grinned. They got to their feet and headed over to Graham, who was putting his armfuls of weapons down on the table.

Carter reached to pick one of the pistols up, and Graham slapped his hand away.

"Don't touch the goods just yet," the blacksmith told him.

Carter raised his hands. "Easy. Have a beer and lighten up."

Graham gave him a skeptical look. "I'm not sure mixing alcohol and weapons is the smartest idea."

"Good thing I'm not smart then, isn't it?" Carter replied. He grabbed a beer and passed it to Graham.

"Looks like I'm in good company." Graham chuckled and took a swig. Carter reached over for a weapon again and Graham slapped his hand without stopping drinking his beer, since he knew Carter would try to get the weapons while he was distracted. The weapons looked too damn cool.

The others all made a big deal of the weapons as they gathered around the kitchen table.

Carter rubbed his hand. "Will you stop slapping me now and show us the goods?"

Massimo stood beside Graham and admired the weapons. "You've outdone yourself, Graham."

Graham was pleased that Massimo approved of his work. "Thank you, Massimo. I've been working on these for years, and there are quite a few upgrades—which is why I've been trying to stop Carter from touching them."

Carter rubbed his hand theatrically. "Oh. Well, you only had to say so."

First, Graham took a wooden spear off the table. It didn't look like there was much to it. It actually looked like the most boring thing there.

Koda inspected the wood. "Nice."

Graham smiled. "That's nothing. Watch this." He tapped

the butt of the spear on the floor and lifted it up off the floor, and instantly 9-inch blades came out of the ends, making it a double-bladed weapon that was perfect for close- to mid-range fighting.

Koda's face lit up, and he held a hand out to Graham. "May I?"

Graham passed it to Koda. "I thought this would be good for you."

Koda took the spear with wide eyes. "Thank you," he told Graham warmly.

"I've got these two sweet pistols for Byrant. I understand that you are very good," Graham said, raising his eyebrow. "I also heard that Willard is a good shot, but when it comes down to it he buckles."

Luckily Byrant wasn't looking or paying attention. His eyes were on the set of guns. He was the drunkest of all of them, and Ryder could understand why, after him flaking so badly in the fight against the Mad. Ryder knew that they had to get that sorted out quickly. It was pointless having the so-called Best Gunslinger in Town if he was too traumatized to fire a weapon.

"I thought you'd like these." Graham held up two shiny axes, and Carter's face lit up like all his Christmases had come at once.

"For me?" Carter cooed, holding the axes against his chest.

Graham rolled his eyes. "Yes, for you."

"I think you're my new best friend. Sorry, Ryder, you're out. Come here, you." Carter clutched Graham in a bear hug, and Graham hugged him back, laughing.

The two men released each other with a grunt. "Was it good for you?" Graham asked with a wink.

"Yeah, I've still got a semi-on." Carter grabbed his crotch and thrust in Graham's general direction. The other men around the table began to laugh.

Graham patted himself on the back. "Looks like my work here is done."

"Well, you can finish me off if you want to," Carter stated.

That got Massimo chuckling, which made Ryder laugh as well.

Graham put his hands in the air. "Not on the first date."

Carter rolled his eyes and asked Ryder, "What's with him? He's such a dick tease."

Ryder shook her head in amusement. "Are you two done with your dick jokes?"

Carter folded his arms and smirked. "I've got more if you want them."

Massimo began collecting the empty beer bottles. "Save them for later, Carter. It's getting late, and we have a big day tomorrow. Let Graham finish his demonstration now."

Carter patted Massimo on the back. "Will do, boss."

Massimo turned to Graham with a resigned sigh. "Graham, why don't you show us what else you have?"

"Sure thing." Graham passed out all the different weapons. He had cool knives, guns, swords, and crossbows, and he gave them all out to the newly-named Merry Men.

Tightwad went for the swords, which were long and impressive. Ryder hadn't expected Tightwad to go for that type of weapon.

He swung them a few times to get the feel and nodded with satisfaction.

Ryder thought he looked strange with his two swords and his colorful sweater, but then she glanced at the table and wondered what weapon *wouldn't* look odd with his outfit. She grinned. Actually, the weapons had nothing to do with it. He was just going to be the funniest looking vampire slayer in the bunker.

"And last, but not least…" Graham held up a cloth-wrapped package.

Ryder's fingers were tingling with excitement, ready to get to hold of her new weapon. She took it from him almost reverently, already certain what was within, and opened the cloth. "It's…it's beautiful…"

"It's more than beautiful," Graham told her. "The arrowheads are made from metal instead of the flint you're used to. No more breakages."

"Thank you, Graham." Ryder giggled as she examined the bow. The craftsmanship was far better than her old bow, and the stronger arrowheads would mean she could be a little less fussy about where she aimed the next time they were fighting. "This is going to make a huge difference."

"That's not the best thing. Watch this." Graham walked over to Massimo's hard alcohol. *I thought he was going to show me something, not just drink more.*

"Do you mind if I steal this?" Graham asked Massimo.

"Be my guest." Massimo was happy to have people drinking in his house. Ryder noticed that Fluffy wasn't walking in a straight line as he came over to the group. He was drunk. Ryder looked down at him, fondly shaking her head as he came to lie down beside her. "Oh, Leandro." She rubbed the spot between his ears. "What is the world coming to? A drunk wolf."

Leandro looked up at her and rolled his eyes.

Graham was ready to continue his demonstration. He lifted the bottle to his lips and then laughed as the fumes made his eyes water. "I'm kidding, relax. This shit's probably too strong for human consumption.". He motioned to Ryder to bring the bow, the arrows, and the bottle of liquor and headed outside, with everyone following close behind him.

He made for his cart and grabbed a few rags from the back. Graham had brought Black Beauty and another horse with a wooden cart to carry all of the weapons, water, and food to the bunker. That way they could save their energy so they would be ready for the fight.

Graham busied himself for a moment. He tore a few strips from a rag and tipped a small amount of the alcohol on them before laying them on the top of a flat rock. He tore more strips from another rag and held one out to Ryder. "Wrap the arrowhead,"

Ryder did as he asked while Graham readied his flint and steel and set the alcohol-soaked rags alight. "Fire?" she asked.

Graham nodded. "You can't do *that* with flint."

Ryder grinned and nocked the arrow. "Cool!"

"I thought you'd like it." Graham smiled.

Ryder dipped her arrowhead into the flame and loosed it at a nearby tree. The arrow *thunked* into the wood with a hiss. "Oh, I like it."

Graham headed over to a bag on the porch while Ryder

went to retrieve her arrow. "I've got extra knives for everyone in here. Also, I brought as many bullets as I had, which wasn't too many. We'll need to use them wisely." Nobody disagreed with that. To have bullets at all was a blessing that they would not waste.

"We need a plan. Let's practice with the weapons, then head back inside and work it out over dinner," Massimo suggested.

Ryder had longed to hear words to that effect for years. Her heart soared with the knowledge that her dream of freedom for the people she cared about was finally coming true. They had the weapons and the team. They would find a way into the bunker and free everyone.

Afana wouldn't live to regret the day he'd kidnapped Ryder.

The gang played with their new toys. Tightwad moved through a few sword techniques, confirming to Ryder that he had experience. She had to stifle a giggle at the juxtaposition of his serious face and his colorful sweater as he sliced through the air like there was a Mad in front of him. Ryder had underestimated Tightwad, and she was glad to have him in the gang.

Carter stood with Byrant, encouraging him to practice. He lined up some potatoes for targets. Carter knew that he needed to get Byrant's confidence up after he'd choked so badly today. There was a fun bit of banter between the two of them. Carter threw his axes at the potatoes, slicing them in two.

Massimo patted Carter on the back. "Carter, you are in charge of chopping vegetables for dinner."

Vicky was using a crossbow, but the arrows went everywhere *except* the target she was aiming for. She spat as she threw it on the ground. "This is a piece of shit."

"Hey!" Graham snapped. He picked up the bow and cradled it as though it were his child Vicky had just cast away.

"It's not as good as my trusty shovel." She retrieved her shovel from where she'd leaned it while she tried the crossbow and swung it up to rest on her shoulder. "At least with this I know I won't miss." She gave it a little swing for emphasis.

Graham watched Vicky's body as she swung. "If you move your hips a little…" Graham reached for Vicky's hips. Vicky stepped back and made to swing the shovel at him. Graham held up his hands. "I just want to show you that if you move your hips just so, you'll get a hell of a lot more power behind the swing, and you won't have as much pain after a fight. Can I?" he asked.

"Any funny business and I'll be swinging this at your head," Vicky said, raising her shovel again.

Graham chuckled. "Funny business? Me? As *if*. Now, place your feet like mine." She copied Graham's stance and readied her shovel. He placed his hands on her hips and tilted them to show her how to pivot to add the power to her swing. "Now try it by yourself."

She swung again, then nodded at Graham. "Not bad. Not bad at all. Can you show me again? This time, your hands can stay on my hips a little longer." She winked.

Graham's hands were on Vicky's hips before she could

change her mind.

"Everyone go grab some food. I'll be in shortly," Massimo told everyone.

Vicky stepped out of Graham's reach. "Come on, you. I know you're...*hungry.*"

"Get a room, you two," Ryder teased.

Vicky grinned. "Ooh, *can* we?" She winked seductively at Graham and strutted into the house.

Massimo stayed on the porch with Fluffy. Even *he* had started to refer to Leandro as Fluffy. Massimo took a seat in the rocking chair and rocked a little. His hand trailed over the new cut marks in the chair arms. He put it down to Afana's men and shook his head at the senseless damage.

Leandro looked up at him and whined softly.

"I know, son. So much has happened over the last forty-eight hours. The murder that wasn't really a murder, the Mad in the Old Dog..." Massimo shook his head sadly. Even though he'd told Leandro he wasn't upset about it, the bar turning into a murder scene had cut him deeply. "Then the fight, and... And you turning into a wolf full-time," Massimo finished softly, stroking Fluffy.

Fluffy rested his nose on Massimo's knee, and Massimo ran his hand through his son's thick white fur. Massimo smiled. Fluffy was the perfect name for him. "I wish you could speak to me right now," he admitted. "I do miss the sound of your nagging."

Fluffy looked up at Massimo. He knew that despite the teasing his Pops was hurting.

Massimo leaned back in the rocking chair. "What can we do?" he asked.

Leandro whined again.

Damn, he was cute when he looked up at Massimo with his large orange eyes. Massimo let out a little laugh and patted Fluffy's head. "You weren't a mind reader when you were a human, so why would you be now you're a wolf?" He traced the scar in the chair arm idly. "I'm not as young as I used to be. Today I felt alive. I have to say, son, *you* looked alive as well. Have we both been hiding our true selves out of fear of the unknown?"

Fluffy tilted his head.

"Ah, you do understand me. I've been thinking. I can't let everyone down tomorrow. How could an old worn-out vampire like me fight a mutant vampire?" He frowned. "I'm thinking I should do something I swore I never would."

His son looked no less confused, but Massimo didn't notice. His mind was on the monumental decision he was coming to.

"I should have stopped Afana years ago before any of this started. I knew what a monster he was back then, and I did nothing. That makes part of those people's captivity my responsibility, and it's about time I took ownership of it. It's time to stop hiding in the shadows and face what my cowardice has brought about." He looked at Fluffy, noticing the glazed look in his son's eyes. "I'm rambling, aren't I? I need to drink human blood and get stronger if I'm going to win against Afana." Massimo paused for a moment.

"What do you think?" he asked Fluffy, "One nod for yes, two for no."

Fluffy nodded.

Massimo ran his hand through Fluffy's fur. "Yes, then." He smiled.

She'd looked good with the flaming arrow, Leandro thought as he watched Ryder. She smiled at him before she loosed it. That woman was hot. *Flaming* hot. Leandro snickered to himself.

He loved watching Ryder, and it was even more fun now because he could see two of her. Now it wasn't creepy because he was a wolf, just staring up at her like a lost puppy.

I'm thirsty again. Leandro had drunk more that night than he had in his whole life. Part of him wished he'd done it more often. He felt more courageous. If he could have spoken he'd have asked Ryder out, although he wasn't sure where he'd take her. The Old Dog would have been the perfect location until all the deaths.

Leandro turned around; everyone was walking back into the house. *Was it something I said?* Leandro chuffed with laughter. *I doubt it. More likely the gas I just let out…*

Massimo took a seat in the rocking chair, and Leandro sat down on the porch next to his Pops.

Leandro rested his head on Massimo's knee, wishing he'd taken more time to just have a few beers on the porch with his Pops while he still could. He closed his eyes as Massimo stroked his head, right…right…

Ahhhh, that's *the sweet spot,* Leandro thought as Massimo rubbed him behind his ear.

Massimo nudged Leandro. "One for yes, two for no."

What?

"Yes, then," Massimo said.

What did I just agree to? Leandro wondered.

3

R yder was having a hell of a lot of fun with her new arrows. They whizzed through the air and landed in the tree trunks with a satisfying thud each time. Her arms were tired from the battle that day and she knew she needed to save her strength for tomorrow's fight, so she decided to call it a day.

When Ryder went to retrieve her arrows, every part of her body ached. The water was leaving her body, and so was the relief it gave her. She'd have to have a few more shots to sleep tonight. She'd aimed for a tree that was far away from the house, which she realized was not the best idea now as she had to go get them. Then again, it was a good thing, since it was giving Massimo and Fluffy time to chat. They were deep in conversation. Well, Massimo was, given that Fluffy couldn't actually speak.

Ryder worked the arrows out of the tree, holding each one up to the moonlight to check for damage. She could make out that the arrows hadn't been blunted by the force of hitting the tree, which was a good thing. She placed her finger on the tip of an arrowhead to double-check that it was nice and sharp.

Ryder slung her bow over her shoulder and headed back to the house. She was hungry now and hoped that everyone in the house hadn't eaten everything while she was out here training.

Ryder turned at a rustle in the trees behind her. With all the extra people, they could do with the meat. She breathed in, and the foul smell of rotting eggs hit her. No animal smelled *that* bad, and Carter was inside, so it wasn't his gassy ass.

It was a Mad.

The branches parted and the Mad zeroed in on Ryder, taking her by surprise. There was no room for her to use her bow, but she *could* use an arrow. Ryder stood her ground and waited until the Mad was almost upon her. The Mad was so close that Ryder could smell death on her breath, and there was a chunk of flesh missing from her cheek that had been bitten away.

Ryder leaned forward, and the Mad's greedy red-glowing eyes widened in anticipation of an easy meal. Ryder took her chance and slammed the arrow point-first into the Mad's ear. The arrow met a little resistance at first, but Ryder pushed through with a few twists.

Ryder grabbed the knife from her belt and sliced the Mad's throat. She wanted to make sure this Mad was dead. She had no remorse for the killing. This Mad may have been a woman once, but whatever part had made her human had been destroyed when the Madness had taken over. They were no longer people. They weren't even animals. Even the supposed monsters were no frightening thing, compared to the hungry husks of humanity that now roamed the Earth.

Ryder jerked her arrow free with a sickening pop and blood sprayed from the Mad's ear. Ryder leaped away from the spray as the Mad fell, but it was too late. Freshly clean Ryder was covered in blood splatter once again. At least she had another reason to have a shower, which wasn't such a bad thing.

Ryder watched the woman fall to the ground and wondered how many more of them were out there. Ryder knew the Madness spread by people biting one another after what she'd seen in the Old Dog, but why *were* people turning Mad? When she'd asked Massimo earlier in the day, he'd thought it was a disease.

She thought back to the Old Dog and the craziness that happened and how it had spread. When one person bit another, they turned and bit someone else, and so on. Ryder thought hard, replaying everything she'd seen in the bar that night. Some things she didn't want to remember, like how many people they'd killed.

The person that had started the killing had seemed normal, well a little drunk, maybe, but they'd had no wounds that she'd seen.

Then there were the people in the mountain settlement where Carter was from. He said they had just started going Mad. *Maybe getting a bite isn't the only way to turn Mad?* That scared Ryder. How were they supposed to fight something they couldn't see?

Her thoughts were broken by the sound of heavy boots approaching. Ryder gripped her arrow, ready to fight again. She relaxed when she saw that it was Massimo and Fluffy.

Massimo grimaced at the bloody corpse of the Mad by Ryder's feet. "I'm so sorry," he apologized. "The alcohol has affected our senses, I'm afraid. Otherwise, we would have heard and come to your aid sooner."

Ryder waved him off. Shit, even *that* hurt. Getting out of bed tomorrow was going to be a bitch. "It's all good. I took care of it." She winked, not wanting Massimo to feel down after the day they'd had. "We need to guard this place against these things. This is the second time they've come by the house. We can take turns."

Massimo nodded. "That's a good idea." He looked like he was ready to fall asleep. "We'll get some of the others on the first rotation." Massimo paused for a moment. "You really do have good ideas, Ryder. Has anyone told you that?"

Ryder grinned at Massimo. "You did, one second ago."

Massimo looked a little confused. "I did? Did I?" he asked in an uncertain tone. Massimo glanced down at his glass. He'd brought his drink to the fight with him.

"Were you planning on getting the Mad drunk?" she teased.

Massimo had a boyish grin on his face. "I think I may have celebrated too much."

"Massimo, do you think the disease is spreading another way?" She quickly filled him in about what she'd seen at both the Old Dog and the mountain settlement. "I think there are two ways of getting the disease. One is to be bitten, we know that. The other… I don't know." Ryder reached up and grasped at the air. "Could it be in the air?"

Massimo sobered instantly. "I had considered that it could be something inside us. The person you described in the Old Dog had been acting oddly for the last few weeks. I thought he'd just been eating magic mushrooms. Come to think of it, that's what Graham had said Andrew's behavior was like. Maybe that could be one of the signs before they changed, then something must have happened in the last few days or weeks to turn the disease on inside of them like a switch had been flicked. Or, as you said, something in the air."

Ryder gulped. "If it's in the air, we're fucked."

Massimo nodded in agreement. "I wish we had the technology from before the WWDE. We'd be able to search the internet to find out how much of the world is affected."

"The internet?" Ryder had heard Massimo mention that word a few times now, but she had no clue what it meant.

Massimo's eyes were misty with recollection. "Oh, how I miss the internet. The internet was a wonderful thing. It had all the world's information on it. You could use it to shop, or even stay in touch with every one of your friends, wherever they were in the world. Or like most people liked to do, spy on their ex's lives on Facebook."

Ryder was lost. Massimo may as well have been speaking another language with all the sense he was making.

Massimo rested his hand on Ryder's shoulder. "Let's get you inside, and get the guys on guard. You must be starving, and there isn't an ounce of fat on you for a reserve. You're just like a supermodel."

Supermodel? Ryder didn't feel super at all as they walked back to the house, Fluffy walked beside Ryder with a little wobble, like he was going to fall to sleep very soon. Ryder hoped she could soon sleep as well. She was exhausted.

Massimo took Ryder's arm to stop her and placed a finger to his lips, and Ryder heard the sound of feet running toward them. They quickly spun to see a group of Mad running at them. Ryder put an arrow to her bow and shouted to the others that there were Mad, but Ryder wasn't sure they'd be able to hear her over the music.

Ryder wasted no time and let the arrows fly into the oncoming Mad. Massimo bared his fangs and ran at the Mad, with Fluffy right beside him.

Fluffy flew through the air and sunk his teeth into a Mad's clothes, which were ripped to shreds as though the Mad had already been in a lot of fights. Ryder knew where they were going, but she wondered where they had come from.

Ryder heard the door behind her swing open and turned to see who'd come to help them. It was all of the Merry Men, and with their new weapons, they were more than ready for a fight.

"Time to test these babies out," Carter yelled, swinging his axes as he ran toward the Mad. The rest of the Merry Men joined Carter with a whoop.

Tightwad swung his swords at a Mad. He chopped off one of the Mad's ears, and it fell to the ground. The Mad went for him, but before he could swing his swords again, Vicky cracked the Mad over the head with her shovel. The Mad stumbled sideways and Tightwad finished him off with another swing, only this time he didn't miss, and the Mad's head rolled.

Koda spun his wooden spear around and clipped a Mad

in the head with the butt. Koda wielded that spear as an awesome weapon, even without the blades.

Graham was annoyed that Koda hadn't used the improvements to the spear. "Koda, press the button," the blacksmith shouted. Koda looked at Graham, confused. "The *button*." Graham pointed to the spear as he stabbed a Mad with his free hand.

Koda fiddled with the spear, then the blade flipped out of the butt and Koda's face lit up. "Thank you, Graham." Koda grinned and used the blade to jab the Mad he was fighting in the eye. The Mad collapsed with blood spurting from its eye socket. "Nice!" Koda enthused.

"Take this, motherfuckers!" Clint yelled around his cigarette as he attacked the Mad with his knives. He slashed them across the stomach and their guts spilled out, but that didn't stop the Mad. They continued to snap at Clint until he sliced their throats when they were close enough.

The Merry Men fought well together, and soon there was a bloody mess of limbs and guts on the ground. The smell of death hung in the air.

"I'm starving," Carter announced, and a few of the others agreed. The bloodbath hadn't put them off food; if anything, the exertion had only made them hungrier. Everyone knew they'd need to keep their strength up if they were going to win their battle against the Mad.

4

Afana had reached Level One at the top of the bunker. His anger was racing through his body like it had never done before. He was a raging bull, and the advisors were his china shop. He grabbed the nearest advisor and lifted him off his feet, then brought him toward his fangs.

Advisor Robert nervously hurried toward Afana. "Afana," Robert yelled. "Please don't! I've noted some of the blood was slow to change, so he might be infected." Afana dropped the man at his feet. If there was a chance the blood was infected, he wasn't going to take it. The advisor didn't know what to do until Robert shooed him away.

Afana stomped over to Robert and scowled. "Level Six have locked themselves in, and now you're telling me that my stock on Level One is potentially infected?" Afana growled.

Advisor Robert nodded. "I am." His voice shook a little and he swallowed, knowing the penalty for showing weakness.

Afana's eyes glowed in response to the fire inside him and his veins began to bulge. "All of these computers and not one of you can open the doors!" Afana's voice echoed through Level One.

Advisor Jones spoke quietly. "We could try restarting the system. That should reset the codes, which would force Level Six open…along with all the other levels."

"Do it," Afana ordered. "But if you're wrong I will drain you."

Advisor Robert had to give Afana a word of caution, "Afana, if all the doors open, the infected could spread the disease to the other levels."

"It's a risk I'm willing to take. I can fend off the cattle." Afana looked almost fondly at Advisor Jones, making him gulp.

Advisor Robert's eyes bulged, and he shook his head at Afana. Afana knew that meant that the disease had shown up in Advisor Jones' blood already. *Even if this works he will be dead,* Afana thought.

Advisor Jones hands were shaking as he placed them over the keyboard and began to type. A short while later he finally stopped typing, his work done. Everyone looked down through the glass floor toward the doors, but it was hard to see them through all the blood.

Afana could see that the panel next to the door had zeros on it. It had gone back to the manufacturers setting. *It worked. Shame he's going to die anyway,* Afana thought.

Advisor Jones turned to Afana and actually smiled. He thought he'd done a good job, dumb cattle. Afana picked up Advisor Jones and threw him down his drop hole. His body tumbled through the floors and crashed down on the locked door of Level Six.

"Who else is infected?" Afana asked Robert, who reeled off two names. Each man went whiter than his lab coat. Afana wasted no time in taking out the trash, just picked each of them up and threw them down his exit.

Now it was time to get the motherfucker on Level Six!

Excitement flooded Afana. All the doors were open, and he could get to Level Six. Afana knew that he'd have to go to each door and input the new codes to lock the doors manually since he didn't trust anyone else to do it. That was just fine since he planned to kill Terrier and anyone else who had been helping him and feast on their blood. Afana paused that thought. He'd feast on the blood once it was given the all-clear.

This got Afana thinking. If the advisors' blood had changed too slowly to show signs of the disease, could the same thing happen to him? Would he become infected? He'd been surrounded by the infected when fighting them. He looked down at his clothes. His black shirt was ripped and had blood all over it, and his hands were redder than they were white.

He was covered in infected blood.

Afana's elation quickly sank away, drowned by the horror of being infected. Revenge would have to wait. Afana left the lab, not for Level Six, but for his quarters on Level One.

He could feel the advisors' eyes on his back as he left. He knew that if he turned around, they would be looking, but he didn't give a shit what they thought. He was going to get this bloody mess cleaned off.

Terrier was confused. First George had told them they were locked in on Level Six and that Afana couldn't open the doors from Level One, then he'd told them that Afana *could* override the doors.

Terrier wanted to shake the right answer out of the advisor. "What are you talking about, George? I thought that we were locked in here."

George looked at Terrier blankly. "We are."

Everyone looked at George, confused.

General Murray was beside Advisor George. "Which is it?" he pressed.

George looked even more confused than everyone else. "What are you talking about?"

"Can Afana open Level Six's door from Level One?" Mama Lou asked Advisor George.

George spoke extra slowly and clearly as though they were all complete dumbasses. "No. I locked us in, and he can't override the door from Level One."

Terrier frowned at George. "I just asked you that question and you said yes. Which is it?"

"What?" Advisor George frowned at them and shook his head. Terrier really wanted to give George a good shake.

Mama Lou waved her hands to calm everyone down. "Terrier, I think you didn't ask the question correctly." Mama Lou repeated the question in a soft tone.

Advisor George squeezed his eyes together, "I *said* no already! He can't get in. We're locked in here!"

Terrier and the others were confused. "How could you make a mistake like that?" Terrier asked.

"I did all right."

Level Six fell quiet for a moment. The people were relieved that they were safe from Afana's rage. Only Terrier knew that they were playing a waiting game now. Their hopes were pinned on Ryder to get to them before the disease broke out down on Level Six, whether they knew it or not.

Terrier was worried that Ryder might not make it back in time. He cursed himself for not going with her. She could have been killed or captured out there. However, leaving the women and children without his protection was not an option. Terrier might not be the sharpest knife in the melee, but he was as loyal as a summer day was long. If Ryder didn't make it back, he would just have to rescue everyone all by himself.

He needed to think of a way to get out of the bunker.

Bodies crashed down onto the ceiling of Level Six, startling the people below. Afana was throwing his advisors from Level One. Their skulls broke on impact, and the drop door was painted with brain matter.

Advisor George screamed, "Why did you have to force me to stay down here? You traitor! I could have helped solve the problem if you'd only let me do my job on the other levels. It's your fault Afana is killing good men."

General Murray rolled his eyes. "Why don't you scream a little louder? That way Afana can hear you."

"There's no point," Advisor George muttered sullenly.

"Why, because he doesn't care?" General Murray shot back.

Advisor George shook his head in defiance. "Because he can't hear me. When I shut the cameras off I had to also take out the speakers, since they are all linked together."

Now General Murray was confused. "Why would anyone link them together?" he asked. "That's the dumbest thing I've ever heard."

Advisor George glared at Murray. "Because that's how the system works."

General Murray grinned. "It doesn't sound too smart to me. I thought advisors were smart. Just my luck to be stuck with one of the dumb ones."

Advisor George took offense to that. "I'm not dumb!"

"Really?" General Murray raised his eyebrow.

The two went back and forth like little kids.

"Stop bickering," Natalie chided from the doorway to the kids' room. "You're supposed to be an example to the kids, and you're acting like kids yourselves." She waved her finger at them sternly.

"Oh, you two just got schooled." Terrier laughed as he walked over to Natalie.

General Murray was annoyed, not at Natalie but at himself. He'd so quickly gone back to his old ways of being a monumental asshole. Murray blushed, embarrassed by his actions. "Sorry, Natalie."

Natalie and the others looked at him in surprise, and he shrugged and smiled back. Natalie started to talk with Terrier. They looked happy.

General Murray remembered when his son Martin was born. He could remember it like it was yesterday even though it had been twenty-two years ago. His son had died too young. Murray glared at Advisor George, who didn't blink as he stared up through the glass floor to Level One.

General Murray looked away from Advisor George. He couldn't let his anger control him, not anymore. He went back to thinking about the day Martin was born.

Annabel was his mother. Murray had loved her, and she'd loved him. She died in childbirth and it broke General Murray's heart, but he hadn't allowed it to show since compassion for women was a sign of weakness on Level Six and weakness would get you killed.

He'd locked away any signs of caring, but Martin'd had a way of unlocking it. His eyes were just like Annabel's, filled with hope. General Murray could get lost in Annabel's eyes when they were able to spend time together, and because of his rank he'd been able to spend all of his free time with her. After Martin was born he lived with the other children on Level Six, but those who were from general or advisor rankings moved up to their level once they turned sixteen.

Martin quickly became Murray's shadow, always by his side even when he wasn't meant to have been. More than a dozen times Murray had punished Martin for it, but it hadn't stopped him. Murray had loved the company of his son, really, but he had to keep him at arm's length because of Afana. If the vampire realized the strength of their bond, he could and would use it against him. He'd seen it happen many times over his life, and he didn't want the same to happen to him and his son—which was why General Murray had sent Martin to work down in Level Six.

As far away from him as possible.

Now Martin was even farther away than he'd imagined,

just when there was a chance of getting out of here. Murray looked for George, but he was gone. *Where's that ginger George now?* Murray wondered. He scanned the area, but he was nowhere to be seen. For fuck's sake!

George wasn't by the exit door trying to open it.

He'd better not have gone after the women. Murray refused to have their blood on his hands. He already had too much of it staining his conscience. Murray did a quick search of Level Six. He didn't want the others to know he'd lost George. What kind of general could lose one scrawny advisor?

General Murray thought for a moment, then headed down the tunnel George was working in before Martin turned Mad. He didn't want to go down there and see his son's body after the women had killed him.

"George, are you down there?" General Murray yelled from the beginning of the tunnel. He knew his voice wouldn't carry far because of the roar of the industrial fans, so he yelled again at the top of his voice.

"What?" Advisor George yelled back.

"What the fuck are you doing?"

"My job!" George snapped. "Come down here and help me."

George must be thinking out his ass again. There was no way Murray was going back down that tunnel, and especially not to help George.

"Leave the cameras," he told him.

"No!" Advisor George screamed. "I'm doing my job!"

General Murray heard metal parts landing on the floor, and the scuffle of George's shoes on the floor. George screamed, and a thud followed.

Then Advisor George huffed, and he came into view with a face as pale as a ghost's and blood down his white lab coat.

George tried to catch his breath and pointed back the way he came. "There's a dead body down there."

Murray looked at George, confused. Why was he making Murray go through this again? What kind of twisted person was he? Then he saw that George was being genuine.

"It's Martin," Murray reminded him.

Advisor George looked around as if he were looking for Martin, then back at General Murray. "Oh, yeah."

Murray frowned. Something wasn't right with George. "Stand over there where I can see you."

George was confused. "I forgot, okay?"

Wrong words.

Murray glared at the advisor. "You forgot that my son died because he was saving you?"

Advisor George twisted at his ginger hair, then tugged on it until it was in his hand.

"What the hell are you doing?" Murray demanded.

George tilted his head, pulling another clump out. "What are you talking about?"

"Your hair. What are you doing to your hair?" Murray snapped.

George looked at his open hands. He turned his hand sideways, and hair fell from it. "I don't feel well," George said. He certainly wasn't acting well.

Murray looked him over skeptically. "You're not going to throw up, are you?"

"Not that type of unwell. This type." He tapped his forehead. Advisor George was a smart man. He didn't need the glowing eyes and crazy physical behavior to know something was going on inside.

"What are you saying?" Murray asked.

George looked at Murray with horror in his eyes. "I'm infected."

"You don't look it. You look like your normal scrawny annoying self." Murray smiled, attempting to lighten the situation.

"I will turn soon. You need to lock me up," George insisted.

Murray was taken aback, but when he thought about it, he realized that George wanted to be locked up to stop them from killing him, not because he was scared of hurting others.

"You need to show me how to unlock the doors first." Murray wasn't going to let their only exit route die.

George looked up at Murray with wide, frightened eyes. "You promise to lock me up and not kill me?" George waited for Murray to reply.

"I promise," Murray assured him.

The two men headed up the stairs toward the door.

"I need your knife. I've lost my tools," George told Murray.

Murray passed him one of his knives and George took the top off the control panel.

The advisor paused. "You need to connect the red and blue wire together." He shook his head. "My mistake, it's the green and orange." He shook his head again. "Why are there so many colors?" He turned to Murray like he knew.

"Which color is it?" General Murray asked.

George tilted his head in confusion. "For what?"

General Murray was unable to contain his frustration. "To get out of here!"

George clapped his hands over his ears. "Stop yelling at me!" George panted. "I can't *think* over all your shouting!"

Murray held his palms up. "Calm down George, I won't shout again. I'm sorry. We just need to know which wires to cross."

"Why would you cross the wires?" he asked in a lost voice.

Murray's heart began to drop. "To get out. Remember?"

George began to laugh hysterically. "We can't get out. We're trapped down here forever." He sat down and started rocking. George had lost it, and there was no coming back from where he had gone.

Murray took George's shoulder to stop him from rocking. "George, snap out of it. You need to tell me what to do to open the door."

He looked up at Murray, big tears rolling down his cheeks. "I can't remember."

Murray wanted to shake the answer from George, but he knew he had to get George into a secure room quickly before he changed. He'd given him his word, and he was going to stand by it.

He placed a hand on the advisor's shoulder. "George, maybe a lie-down would help you come up with the answer."

"To what question?" George asked. Murray knew in his bones that he would never get the answer from Advisor George.

He guided George to one of the rooms a couple of

doors down from Vera's. He found it strange how quickly they'd gotten used to the groans from Vera and the banging on the door as she tried to escape. It just became…well, another sound.

He opened the door, and George went inside meekly. "I am feeling a little tired. Wake me when it's time to leave." He walked to the bed, laid down, and closed his eyes.

"Good night, George." Murray closed the door. There was no lock on the outside, but he needed to lock him in because everyone was at risk if he turned.

Peter arrived and walked over to Murray. "What are you doing?" he asked, raising his eyebrow, and then looking at the door. "Who's behind the door?"

Peter went to the door and opened it. He saw George on the bed in the same position as Murray had left him. "Lazy ass, taking a nap. Fuck *that*." Peter made to go in and drag George out of bed, but Murray stopped him.

"Don't do it," General Murray told him. Peter looked down at the hand on his shoulder, and Murray quickly removed it. Murray closed the door again. "He thinks he's infected."

Peter grimaced. "I can't say I like the whiny little prick, but I wouldn't wish that ending on anyone. Actually, that's not true. I wish it on one person—Afana."

Murray nodded in agreement. "Me too. I think we all do. I bet that bastard is the only one who can't get it."

Peter shrugged. "Too true. I bet no one could bite through his tough skin." They both winced at the thought.

"His skin is like the bottom of an old man's foot, all dry and crusty," Peter added, and the men turned up their noses at the thought.

"I'm glad I'm done being his bitch," Murray admitted.

Peter patted him on the back. "About time." Both men nodded, sharing a moment. Finally, they could admit how they really thought about Afana without the fear of him killing someone they cared for and then them.

Murray didn't know how long their newfound freedom would last, but he would enjoy it while he could.

Everyone had gathered food from Massimo's fridge and cupboards. The kitchen was going to be empty soon with all these hungry people to eat him out of house and home.

"We need to watch over the house. We can work on guard shifts," Ryder informed the group. They all agreed.

"Willard and I can take the first watch," Javier offered. "Then there will be less chance of him falling asleep and me getting attacked by a wolf again." He looked pointedly at Fluffy.

Fluffy paid him no attention. He was too busy searching under the table for scraps of food that had been dropped. Ryder thought, *I'll have to make him a plate of food.* It looked as though Fluffy had taken Leandro over while he was drunk. Ryder couldn't imagine Leandro doing anything like that if he was himself since he was such a clean person.

Ryder remembered the two of them dancing in Koda's

kitchen while they were cooking for everyone, and the thought of Leandro's hands on her waist warmed Ryder. She used to dance with the little kids in the bunker while Natalie would sing, and they would laugh, but this was different. She'd never danced with a man before, a man had never been that close.

"There's enough of us for two-hour watches. That way everyone can get a decent amount of sleep."

Everyone agreed with Ryder's plan, and Javier closed the door behind him and Willard.

"Where do you think they came from?" Ryder pondered.

Everyone was silent for a moment, "I didn't recognize any of those Mad," Massimo admitted. "They weren't from Pinewood."

"They weren't from the mountain settlement, either," Carter added.

Dustin coughed. "I knew a few of them," he informed the group soberly. "They were from Darkwell." Darkwell had been overrun yesterday, but there had been a handful of people left. It appeared that the Madness had taken the rest of them.

Massimo rested his hand on Dustin's shoulder. "I'm sorry."

"I'm going to clean up." Ryder left the kitchen to shower once again.

When she returned, everyone was gathered in the kitchen. Carter hardly looked up from his food, just nodded and went back to eating. Ryder knew they were waiting for her. She had to figure out their next steps, and she was ready. She'd been waiting for this day for years. She couldn't wait to pay Afana back for all the years he had stolen from her life and others.

Ryder sat down and pushed the chair under the table. The meeting was in session, and all eyes were on her. "Thank you all for agreeing to help. For too many years Afana has been free to destroy hundreds of people's lives, but we are going to change that. I'm not going to lie to you, it's not going to be easy. But Afana has never come up against determination like ours before!" Ryder paused to take a breath, and the group filled the gap with cheers.

"Graham, can we bring the horses to pull the cart for the weapons and other stuff?" Ryder asked Graham.

"Sure, as long as me and Carter can ride Black Beauty together," Graham said, winking at Carter. Those two had quickly built a boy-crush on one another.

Carter winked back.

"Whatever floats your boat." Ryder chuckled. "Okay, this is the plan." Ryder paused to make sure that everyone was listening. "The bunker is made up of six levels. The top level is Level One, where Afana lives and the advisors work. First, we'll need to get past the two guards, Tank and Knuckles, or possibly two others, who won't have weapons. Then there will be the generals, who will have guns. Their job is to guard the bunker, mainly to make sure people don't try to escape. They won't be expecting an attack, so we should take advantage of that. The entrance leads to Level One. We need to get to the lowest level, Level Six. We could take out the guards as we move through the levels. Well, until they notice us. We should try to save the bullets until after we've been spotted. We need to be ruthless, silent killers. I want those fuckers to suffer." Ryder banged her fist on the table, and the men nodded with gritted teeth. *So far, so good.*

Massimo gave her one of his twinkling smiles. "That sounds easy enough."

Ryder shook her head. "Yes, but then we have a problem with the cameras on Level One where the advisors are stationed. They watch the whole bunker."

"What's a camera?" Carter asked.

A few of the others listened closely since they didn't know what a camera was either.

Ryder did her best to explain, although she didn't really understand how they worked. "There are these little boxes around the bunker that capture moving pictures of everything that's going on, then somehow they transfer the images to another box with a screen to watch it." Only Massimo appeared to understand, and Ryder was sure he was suppressing a chuckle at her description. "It doesn't matter. Just be aware that the cameras are there. Also, the floors are glass so Afana can watch everyone."

Massimo looked disgusted at what he was hearing. "He was watching you all the time? Like you were ants in an ant farm."

Ryder nodded. "Yes. The only places without glass floors are the tunnels off the main sections. These tunnels are where we sleep, the hygiene area, and where we prepare food and do maintenance. The cameras caught everything there. Well, until I broke some of them." Ryder smiled.

Carter held his hand up for a high five, which Ryder didn't return since his hands were covered in food. "Nice."

Koda's face was solemn. "Tell me if I have this right. We have to get to the camera station on Level One, in case the cameras aren't off. That's where Afana the monster vampire is. Then move through the five levels to get to the lowest and free the women and children. Then get them back through all the levels and out to freedom?"

Ryder nodded.

Koda shrugged. "Sounds easy enough."

Koda's attitude took Ryder by surprise. So far both he and Massimo thought they could do this with no problem.

"I'll take care of the cameras. They'll be hooked up to the computers." Massimo's IT skills from his former life would come in useful. It had been a long time since he'd tinkered with computers, since after the World's Worst Day Ever had happened, there were no more computers and no need for an IT guy.

Fluffy howled as if to say, "I'm coming as well!"

"Perfect bit of father son bonding time. After that, we'll deal with Afana. Unless we come across him first! Then we'll take him down, and the bunker will be ours!" Massimo spoke like it was going to be a walk in the park.

Ryder wished it was going to be as easy as Massimo thought, but she wasn't going to dampen their spirits now. "Great! Then the rest of us will take on the bunker. I'll go into more detail on how we're actually going to do that."

Ryder talked until her throat was dry, then took another sip and carried on. They had a plan, and each of their skills would play a key role in overthrowing the bunker. Each man was as vital as the next if they were to have a chance of coming out of that place alive.

Ryder raised her glass. "We'll set them all free. To freedom!"

"Cheers to that!" Carter raised his glass, and everyone else did the same.

"Here's to ripping a new asshole in any fucker who crossed Ryder and the other women in the bunker!" Carter cheered.

Ryder knew he meant Natalie as the other women. *"Fuck, yeah!"* Ryder agreed.

6

Hours had passed, and the moon had risen high in the sky while the gang had been fine-tuning their plan. They could all do with a bit of relief after the events of the last few days, and Massimo knew just what they needed.

"Wait till you guys see this." Massimo's face lit up as he pointed to a big black box in the living room right in from of the sofa—the TV.

He turned it on and tapped his lips with a finger in thought. "What shall I put on?" He looked at Fluffy mischievously. Leandro would have stopped him for sure. "The movies I'm about to show you are our history before the World's Worst Day Ever." Massimo looked through his DVD collection, trying not to laugh. Tomorrow he'd tell them it was all made up, but tonight he'd have a bit of fun with them.

Everyone had gathered around the TV. Only Kelvin had seen it before, and he knew that the large selection of movies didn't represent reality. Massimo had played the same trick on him until Leandro had put an end to it, but there was no one to stop Massimo this time. Massimo gave Kelvin a look to as if to say, "don't say a word." Kelvin wasn't going to. He actually thought it would be funny as well, so he grinned back at Massimo.

"Why don't you show them *Star Wars?*" Kelvin suggested. Everyone on the sofa turned to face Kelvin, then back to Massimo as the two went back and forth with different movie titles. Those that were sat on the floor tried to watch the pair, but after a bit their necks hurt.

"I think we'll save Star Wars for another day. We'll need to do that in a marathon Sunday-style watching." Massimo pondered for a moment. All of his favorite movies were whizzing through his head like was watching a countdown of the best movies of all time—*Die Hard, Monty Python and the Holy Grail*, any of John Wayne's westerns.

"It's not that exciting," Carter complained as he stared at the blank TV.

After today they needed a comedy. Massimo looked at his Will Ferrell collection and pulled out *Talladega Nights*. He could screw with their heads another day on world history.

He played the DVD, and everyone in the room fell silent, completely in awe. Massimo loved watching people's faces the first time they saw the TV. They were mesmerized and laughed at all the right parts. Massimo was happy with his selection. The day's events had been washed away by a few hours of laughter, just like in the good old days. The only thing missing was popcorn.

Everyone was tired, and the adrenaline had left their

bodies once the movie had ended. The alcohol and food had made them sleepy.

Massimo got up from the couch. "Ryder, you can take Leandro's room. I'm sure he wouldn't mind."

Leandro had snuck off to his room earlier. *Tired little pup*, Ryder thought, smiling to herself.

"Vicky, you can take the guest room." Massimo walked over to Vicky. "I'll show you where it is. The rest of you can crash in the living room, I'm sorry I don't have enough beds for everyone. There are blankets in the cupboard." Massimo pointed to the cupboard, so everyone knew which one he meant. "We need to get up in a few hours, so I recommend everyone gets some sleep. I'll wake you when it's time."

Ryder wondered what song he'd be singing in the morning. Maybe instead of *Here Comes the Sun*, it would be something more like, *Here Comes the Merry Mother-fuckers Who Are Going to Rip You a New Asshole*. It didn't really rhyme, but Ryder thought the sentiment was spot on.

Everyone said their goodnights and headed to the different rooms in the house.

Carter and the other guys got comfortable on the sofa, chairs, and floor using the blankets and pillows for makeshift beds. None of them complained about their sleeping arrangements. They were a good team.

Ryder was shocked that she'd been able to find so many great people. All her life, she'd been surrounded by people who would cheerfully kill her to get what they wanted. There were good people as well, like Terrier, Mama Lou, Natalie, and all the people on Level Six. Ryder couldn't wait until her two groups of friends were together, and that would happen soon.

Massimo walked over to Ryder after showing Vicky her room for the night. "What type of plant is that?" Ryder said as she pointed to a green plant that had sharp spikes on it. She poked a finger at it, and the spike broke her skin it was like a tiny dagger.

"It's a cactus. They normally grow in deserts. I've had this one," Massimo paused as he thought, "for years, since before the World's Worst Day Ever."

"I'd like to learn more about the World's Worst Day Ever when you have a free moment," Ryder asked.

Massimo greeted that question joyfully. "Of course. There is so much history I'd love to fill you in on." Massimo smiled. He was as happy to tell Ryder as she was to learn.

Ryder smiled back at Massimo. "I would like that very much, and thank you, Massimo, for everything."

"It's the least I can do. We can chat about it on the walk to the bunker tomorrow." He smiled fondly at Ryder. "I've been meaning to speak to you privately," Massimo told her quietly.

The two decided to go outside and sit down on the porch since everyone was settling down for the night.

Ryder's finger trailed over the knife marks in the chair arm. "I'm sorry about Sergei and Yegor breaking into your house. And about this." Ryder touched the scar.

Massimo waved his hand. "Don't worry about that. It's just *stuff* and you weren't the one who broke in, so you have nothing to be sorry about." He smiled warmly, and Ryder knew he meant it.

"Thank you, Massimo. Why did you want to speak to me?" Ryder asked.

Massimo hesitated for a moment. "I've been thinking about what you said, and I think you're right. Afana was always a monster, and you need a strong vampire by your side to win this fight."

Ryder couldn't believe her ears. She leaned forward. "What are you saying, Massimo?"

"I think I need to take you up on your offer," Massimo replied.

Ryder knew he was dancing around the words. He needed her blood to get stronger, and she needed him to be strong. "You need my blood."

Massimo nodded.

Ryder flipped her wrist over, revealing her veins to Massimo as she rested it on the arm of the chair. "Take it. I need your help. We have to free them at any cost." *Even if it's my life,* she thought.

Massimo started to fidget. He was feeling uneasy about this, and Ryder didn't want him to back out. She knew the struggle Leandro had to get him to drink rabbit blood, and this was even worse. She needed to act fast before he changed his mind. "I can pour it in a glass, and you can pretend it's wine." Ryder smiled and got to her feet like this decision was already made.

Ryder left Massimo on the porch and went into the house. The house was quiet, except for the men snoring and the low volume of the TV.

She grabbed a glass and made sure it was clean, then found a rag to stop the bleeding. She didn't want to bleed out. Then she picked up the new knife Graham had given her. She'd hoped the first cut wouldn't be on her. She made a cut on her forearm, and made sure every precious drop went into the glass. Ryder wasn't sure how much was blood he needed, so she filled the glass. As soon as Ryder started to feel dizzy, she bandaged the cut. Depending on the results, Ryder knew that she may have to repeat the whole thing again in the morning, and she was willing to do it.

Massimo instantly turned to Ryder when she stepped through the door and onto the porch. His eyes went to the glass.

He shook his head, "I don't know if I can do this. I'm not one of those vegetarians who pretends to not eat meat, and when no one is around, they sneak a chicken drumstick or a steak. Meat nauseates me, and the smell of blood is twisting my stomach. I really think I'm going to be sick."

Ryder laid a gentle hand on the vampire's shoulder. "Massimo, I need your help. Just think of it as one of your new cocktails." Ryder placed the glass on the table by his chair. "I'll leave you to decide. Good night, Massimo, and thank you again. For everything." Ryder left Massimo on the porch to make his decision.

7

Afana showered until the water ran clear instead of red. Then he'd changed, and now he was ready. He'd thought about his plan of attack, which wasn't usual for him. Normally, he would attack first and think later. Actually, that wasn't true. He wouldn't think later, either. He was more of a "live in the moment" person, and the present moment was a very tense one. He could feel that he needed some blood since he wasn't at full strength, but he wasn't going to drink from just anyone for a quick fix.

Afana was ready to bring his bunker back to order. He planned to get Terrier out of Level Six and make him into a memorable example to show others who were thinking about being traitors what awaited them. This time he was going to make sure that the infected didn't get too close to him, and make sure he killed them. He wasn't going to let any of those jerks bite him while his back was turned.

Afana walked into the lab and spoke to Advisor Robert. "Any updates on the test results?"

"None of the other Advisors' bloodwork has shown signs of infection yet, which is good news. However, I need more time before you feed on them just to be sure."

"And my blood?" he demanded. Advisor Robert cringed a little, and Afana knew that it wasn't a good sign. "Tell me," he ordered through gritted teeth.

Advisor Robert spoke quickly. "Your blood has shown signs that you can be infected by the disease. With a large amount of the infected blood, you will become infected also." Advisor Robert backed away from Afana slightly.

Afana wasn't a person who could control his temper. He was fighting his every instinct simply because he needed to keep Advisor Robert alive long enough to create a cure. "Keep running tests and see if there are any changes. Is there a cure?" Afana asked.

This time Advisor Roberts didn't pause, since he knew how much that annoyed Afana. "I will continue to run the tests. We aren't anywhere close to a cure. It will take time." Advisor Robert admitted, hoping that Afana, as a scientist himself, would understand that cures could happen in a few days or years, and sometimes never.

Afana sighed. "We need to work on containing the infected and getting the cameras back up."

Advisor Robert was glad of the opportunity to redirect Afana's thoughts. He gave him an update on the bunker. "The generals are on Level Five doing a sweep. There were a lot of them killed in the last big fight. Once their sweep is completed, we'll move them up onto Level Four."

Only Levels Four and Five, Afana thought with relief. "Have there been any breakouts on Levels Three and Two?" he asked. That was where the generals and the advisors lived, and they didn't only house men. The families of the generals and advisors also lived there. Afana had done that so he could keep an eye on them, and let them build relationships he could use against them at any point. Their bonds with their loved ones were their weakness.

Advisor Robert shook his head. "None yet."

"Interesting. Why not on those levels yet?" Afana questioned, then he thought about Level Six. He hadn't seen any evidence of a breakout down there, either. "Could those who have not been outside have less of a chance of catching the disease? Is it airborne?"

"But the advisors on Level One had the disease, Afana, and those men have never been outside. It is random. It has to be."

Afana thought about the two most important pieces of information Robert had given him. If he got bitten, he could be infected, and they didn't have a cure. Afana's bunker was a ticking time bomb that could go off at any moment. He didn't like that idea. He needed to stop the outbreak before it got any worse.

***

Mama Lou walked over to General Murray, Peter, and Terrier, who stood next to one of the private doors. She looked around and noticed that Advisor George was missing, then looked at the exit. It was still closed, so that was a good sign.

"Where's Advisor George?" Mama Lou asked.

General Murray gestured at the locked door.

"Why is he in there?" Mama Lou questioned.

"Because he's infected," Murray told her.

Mama Lou looked at the men in horror. "Why is he still alive?"

"He's not actually succumbed yet. His mind started to go, and he knew that he was going to turn soon," General Murray informed Mama Lou.

Mama Lou smiled sadly. "So the rat was smart, after all?"

Murray nodded. "Appears that way. But not at the end. He couldn't remember how we get out of the bunker. I tried everything, but he just couldn't remember. It was like it had been erased from his memory."

"There has to be a way to get it out of him." Mama Lou moved toward the door and put her hand on the pole that was wedged under the handle to stop George from getting out. Peter placed his hand on top of Mama Lou's to stop her.

"It's not safe for you in there," Peter told her gently.

Mama Lou knew he was right. If Advisor George wasn't infected, Mama Lou could have snapped him like a twig. But he was, and Mama Lou wasn't able to fight that.

"I'll go in." Peter moved to grab the pole, then banging came from the other side of the door, and he pulled his hand back. The banging didn't stop. It was in sync with Vera's banging, which everyone had gotten used to. Weird groans came through the door.

They all looked at one another. It was too late. Advisor George was completely gone, taking with him the way for them to get out of the bunker. The three of them fell silent for a moment as they watched the door bounce with each pound of George's fists. He was definitely stronger now the disease had taken over.

They would have to find another way to get the Level Six door open.

"Quick, get out … Get out!" Natalie yelled as she flung open the kids' room door.

General Murray, Terrier, and Peter ran over to Natalie as the kids came running out of the door. Their faces were ghost-white and terrified.

Not a kid, not a kid. The thought ran through Terrier's mind like a poisoned arrow.

A woman leaped through the air right at Terrier— Evelyn Young. She had been helping Natalie with the kids, and now she was stronger than Terrier had expected. She knocked Terrier to the ground, then lunged to bite down on his neck.

General Murray grabbed Evelyn and threw her off Terrier, but he wasn't as strong as Afana and Evelyn sprang back to her feet.

Evelyn's hair was disheveled, she had a crazy look in her red glowing eyes, and her teeth snapped at the air as if she were practicing biting.

The center area of Level Six was filled with potential meals. She darted toward the nearest person before that person could react. It was one of the men who had been trapped down here when Afana had put the bunker on lockdown. Evelyn's teeth chomped down before she was stopped. The man screamed in pain as Evelyn tore a chunk of flesh from his neck.

People ran away in horror and kids cried out in fear.

Samantha fell onto the ground when she stumbled over her own feet.

Evelyn sprang for the next victim, and General Murray launched into action. He reached for his weapon to shoot Evelyn but it wasn't there. Mama Lou had it.

And Mama Lou didn't have a clue how to use it.

Murray couldn't let Evelyn get Samantha. He would have to take her on with his bare hands. He dived between Samantha and the thing that had been Evelyn.

Peter scooped Samantha up and passed her to Mama Lou. Mama Lou shoved the gun into Terrier's hand, but Terrier didn't know what to do with it.

Evelyn let out a blood-curdling growl and went for General Murray. He punched Evelyn in the jaw and her head swung sideways, then she bolted off in search of easier prey.

Terrier, Peter, and General Murray went after Evelyn, and the pipe-wielding women looked on in horror. Evelyn was their friend, but they wouldn't let her hurt the kids. The women formed a protective shield around the children.

Evelyn had bitten one more man before the three of them got to her. She was fast, tearing a strip from one and quickly moving onto the next victim. Bright red blood ran down her face as she lunged for her next victim.

The men had failed to keep Level Six safe, but now the killing had to stop.

"Murray." Terrier passed General Murray the gun.

General Murray couldn't get a clear shot. Evelyn darted back and forth. "I need her to hold still."

That wasn't that easy, but Terrier was going to stop her.

Evelyn was biting her next victim when Terrier came up behind her and picked her up in a bearhug. She thrashed her head around trying to bite Terrier's arms, but he moved them out of the way as he tried to keep his hold on her.

Terrier spun Evelyn to face General Murray. "Shoot her," he pleaded.

"I might shoot you," General Murray fretted.

Terrier really didn't want to get shot, and he didn't want the killing to carry on. "Shoot her *now*." Terrier let go of Evelyn and ran to the side.

General Murray shot Evelyn right in her glowing red eye. Blood poured from it like a red tear, pooling on the floor beneath her head.

8

____

Ryder headed to Leandro's room. She was totally exhausted. Fluffy was curled up on the bed, and he looked so cute. She took off her boots, relishing the fact that she felt safe enough to do so.

She slipped under the blanket, trying not to wake Flurry. Her eyes were heavy, and she let herself fall asleep.

What the fuck! Sergei and Yegor were in Leandro's room and their eyes were glowing like they'd gone Mad. Did I not two-tap them? Ryder sprang out of her bed and went to grab her knife from her pants, but they weren't there. Ryder had put them to the side before she'd gone to sleep, but they were no longer there. Had someone snuck into Leandro's room and taken them? Who would do that?

Sergei and Yegor were coming for her. Their arms were out in front of them, and they were groaning. Ryder punched Sergei, and her hand went right through his head and came out the other side. What the fuck? She pulled her hand back, and blood oozed out with it.

She did the same to Yegor, punching until their skulls had turned to putty. Her fist made gaping holes in the men's heads, but they were still coming for her. She jumped onto Leandro's bed and screamed for help.

Ryder felt wetness on her face, breaking her from the darkness of the nightmare. Fluffy was leaning over Ryder licking her face. *Gross!* Ryder rolled away, and Fluffy stopped licking and looked at her. He'd had to wake her from her nightmare, and how else could he have done it?

"Thanks, Fluffy." Ryder felt weird calling him Leandro after being licked awake. Fluffy wagged his tail. She was still able to communicate with Leandro even if he couldn't talk. "I knew you'd still be in there, Leandro. Next time, could you make it less wet?" She wiped the saliva from her face.

It was still dark outside. Ryder looked at the clock. She'd been asleep for a few hours, but she needed more sleep for tomorrow.

Ryder laid back and stroked Fluffy for comfort. The dream had felt too real. The fight had only happened a few hours ago, and because of that Ryder was replaying every image in her head, right down to the looks on Sergei's and Yegor's faces before she killed them. Ryder didn't feel guilty for doing it since it had been them or her. Besides, she'd known those men for years, and she'd never call them friends. Ryder wondered if tomorrow she'd have to fight off some of her friends in the bunker.

What if someone she cared about couldn't see that Ryder and her friends were doing the right thing? Some people had spent their whole life living in the bunker. Would they even *want* to be free? The worries consumed

Ryder for a second, but she quickly squashed them with thoughts of setting the kids free. Most of them had never been outside the bunker. Their lives had been stolen from them before they'd even begun, just as Ryder's had. If some didn't want her help, that would be fine with Ryder. She was there to free those who wanted to leave.

Ryder closed her heavy eyes once again. Sergei and Yegor weren't going to haunt her dreams anymore. None of the scum from the bunker would.

Only the thoughts of setting everyone free would play in Ryder's dreamscape.

Carter heard a shuffle behind him. "Dude, you have to see this. It's fucking *crazy.*" Carter was deep into *The Empire Strikes Back.* He loved the TV, and couldn't stop watching it. Massimo had the best selection of movies he'd ever seen, which was easy to say since he'd never seen a movie before he'd met Massimo. *The Fast and the Furious* was his favorite. Massimo had told him that there were eight movies but that he only had the first one, and that the abandoned mall would have the rest. The abandoned mall sounded like the best place Carter had ever heard of.

Carter glanced over his shoulder when he realized the person wasn't coming to sit with him. "Your loss. Close the door you're letting a draft in." He turned to see who it was. "*Oh shit!*" He jumped up from the sofa when he saw that it was Javier, and his eyes were glowing red. "Fuck fuck *fuck!*"

Carter was aware of the change before Javier, who looked at him blankly. Carter took advantage of Javier's brief moment of confusion to look around for his axes. They were on the dining room table where he'd left them when they'd cleaned the table after eating. Javier stood between them, blocking him from getting them.

"*Mad!*" Carter yelled at the top of his voice, and the others jerked at the rude awakening. He also kicked the feet of the people closest to him.

Javier lurched toward Carter, but the couch blocked him. He banged into the couch, his mind so consumed by the need to feed on flesh that he didn't register the idea of walking around it to get at Carter.

The others sprang to their feet, horrified that one of their friends had gone Mad.

Javier didn't have any cuts or bites, and he didn't have the awful smell yet. He looked very much like himself except for the glowing red eyes and slack, needful expression as he grasped fruitlessly for Carter. There wasn't even any blood on his clothing.

Graham worked his way slowly around to Carter. "What the fuck happened to him? It doesn't look like he was bitten." He was right; there were no signs that he'd been bitten. Everyone glanced at one another, even more scared now.

The movement brought Javier to his senses, and he shuffled forward with his arms outstretched as he grasped for the nearest person to bite. The moment Javier moved they all rushed around to the table, stirring their Mad friend into action. Everyone grabbed their weapons quickly as Javier darted around the sofa to get them.

However, the Madness had Javier now, and he wasn't

going to stop even with everyone pointing their weapons at him.

"Javier, stop!" Willard had his knives pointing right at Javier. Javier paused for a brief second as though he recognized his friend, but that wasn't the case. It was more that Koda was closer to him and weaponless.

Willard snagged one of the loaded guns from the table. He took the safety off and aimed at Javier's head. "Javier, *stop!*" he cried again, to no effect. Willard sighed and steadied his hands.

"Don't shoot him there," Carter pleaded.

"Where would you like me to shoot him?" Willard snarked. "I don't want him to suffer. He was my friend."

Carter pointed at the TV. "I meant don't shoot him *there*. I need to see what happens at the end of the movie." He waved his arms to get Javier's attention. "Javier, dinner is this way."

The others looked at Carter as though he'd lost his mind.

"Here, Javier, there's a good Mad…" Carter drew him away from the precious television one step at a time. "Come on, Javier. You know you want a bite of my tasty flesh. Koda's all bones; you don't want to eat him." Carter moved closer to Javier, who pivoted and lurched at Carter since he was now the closest. Carter's plan of getting him away from the TV had worked a little too well. Javier was in front of Carter within seconds.

Carter dodged Javier's snapping teeth and shoved his grasping hands away.

"Duck," Willard yelled.

Carter did just that. You listen to a man with a gun when he tells you to duck.

"I'm sorry," Willard apologized as he squeezed the trigger and let the bullet fly into Javier's head. Javier's gaping mouth filled with blood as his last gurgled breath came out in ragged starts. "See you on the other side," Willard finished.

The room fell silent as Javier collapsed to the floor.

Then the door flew open. Everyone pointed their weapons in that direction and then dropped them, since it was Ryder and Fluffy. They'd been woken by the gunshot. Ryder was armed and ready to fight. A door creaked on the other side of the house, and Vicky appeared with her shovel in her hand. Her hair was as wild as she looked. All these cool weapons, and she still had the shovel.

Carter grinned. "Nice of you three to join us, although we could have done with you a few moments ago,"

Ryder walked barefoot toward Javier. "What happened to him?"

"The Madness got him," Carter told her.

Ryder scanned until she spotted Willard by the door. "Willard, how did he get the Madness?" Ryder asked. "Was he bitten? Are there more out there?"

Willard came in and placed the gun back on the table before dropping onto a chair. He stared at the gun, unable to look at his friend's lifeless body.

Ryder walked over and took a seat beside Willard. The others gathered around the table to find out what had actually happened.

Willard held his face in his hands for a moment, then looked at them all with guilt-stricken eyes. "We had split up. I was watching the front of the house, and he was watching the back. I was determined not to fall asleep again, not after last time and what happened to Javier. I was walking around to keep myself awake when I heard him talking to someone. I thought it was one of you guys so I ran around to see, but there was no one there. He was talking to himself." Willard paused and looked around at everyone listening intently to him. "I asked him who he was talking to."

"What did he say?" Carter asked.

Willard shook his head. "He said *I* was the one going crazy, that I was hearing things. I thought he must have been right because I was worn out, like my mind was playing tricks on me or something?" Willard shrugged. "I walked back around the front of the house again. When I did the loop around back he wasn't there so I circled the house again, but he'd gone. That was when I came into the house, to tell him to get his ass back outside. But I can't now, can I?" He finally looked at Javier's body.

Ryder listened to everything Willard had said. "So he wasn't bitten?"

Willard shook his head. "I don't think he was. He would have told me if he'd been bitten earlier in the day. There were no Mad bodies outside that he'd fought off." Willard met Ryder's eyes as he searched for the answer. "He just turned. I wish he *had* been bitten. Then there would at least be an explanation."

Everyone was silent for a moment. Ryder had feared that this would be the case after she and Massimo had spoken about it. The mystery surrounding Javier's infection proved that there was an invisible killer among them.

Maybe the Madness had been there all along, just lying dormant. But why now?

"I'm sorry, Willard." Ryder rested her hand on his arm, which was cold. "You can take Leandro's bed if you like and I'll go on watch," Ryder offered.

Willard shook his head, "I can't sleep now. Besides, the fresh air will do me some good." He got to his feet.

"I'll come with you, mate." Carter put his arm around Willard's shoulder, and Ryder smiled at him. He really was a good guy. They all were.

Carter stood in the doorway for a moment, then stepped back into the house and pointed. "Massimo is one lucky fucker. Javier must have turned as he entered the house or he would have gone after Massimo. He's dead to the world out here."

Ryder and the others left the house to see what Carter was talking about. Massimo was still sitting in the rocking chair on the porch. *Was he still deciding whether to drink my blood?* Ryder wondered. He was asleep, and the glass was empty.

He'd drunk it.

Ryder looked at him for a moment. He looked like he had fewer wrinkles, and it was hard to tell in the light, but she could swear some of the silver was gone from his hair. She rubbed her eyes. *It was working. Maybe that was why he hadn't woken up with the commotion and the gunshot... Or maybe I'm just seeing what I want to see.*

There was a little chill in the air. *Massimo must be cold,* Ryder thought. She wondered whether to wake him and turned to Carter. "Carter, could you keep an eye on him? I don't think we should wake a vampire." She shrugged.

Everyone agreed with her. Even Fluffy nodded his shaggy head.

Carter shrugged. "Yeah, totally not a good idea to wake a vampire. I don't know much about them, but Massimo is totally a badass when he's a vampire. I saw him fight with the locals."

Ryder went back into the house for a blanket. She carefully wrapped it around Massimo, trying not to wake him.

Carter and Willard stayed outside to watch the house and Massimo, and the others headed back inside.

Ryder thought about what had just happened, and how quickly things could change. "I think we should check Javier's body for bites and see once and for all whether he was infected by a bite. We need to know what we're up against. If we can turn into one of them at any point, that's some scary shit. Then after that, Vicky, can we borrow your shovel? We'll give him the burial a true warrior deserves." Ryder bowed her head soberly at the thought of digging a grave for one of her new friends. She wished Carter were here to liven up the moment. Maybe that was why he'd left with Willard; because he knew he couldn't.

Vicky's usual snarky demeanor was absent. She patted Ryder on the shoulder a little awkwardly. "Sure. I'll start digging."

Ryder had to hold her emotions in check. "Thank you, Vicky."

Vicky nodded wordlessly and left.

They inspected the body, and Willard was right—there were no bites on Javier.

The Madness was spreading another way.

9

Massimo stretched his legs. He'd fallen asleep in the chair on the porch, and his bones were aching a little from sleeping awkwardly. The sun wasn't up yet but would be soon, so he needed to wake the others.

Today was going to be a day he wouldn't forget. He was going to stand up for those who were weaker than him. He got to his feet and stretched his arms out above him. "That feels better." Massimo looked at the empty glass on the table by his chair. *I drank Ryder's blood, and I don't feel like draining anyone.* Massimo was relieved. He'd been very afraid that the blood would change him, force him into becoming a monster like the Forsaken of old.

His hands went to his face, which felt smooth. Then he looked at his hands, which were less wrinkled. Massimo looked at his reflection in the window. It was hard to see clearly, but he totally looked younger, taller, and more handsome.

Giddy, Massimo winked at himself and headed to the bathroom to check himself out properly.

Ryder heard a commotion in Massimo's living room. It sounded like everyone was talking very quickly. The sun hadn't risen yet, but Ryder knew it was time for them to go since they'd planned to get to Afana's bunker just after the sun was up. That way they'd have most of the day.

Fluffy pawed at the door, asking Ryder to let him out.

"Sorry, Fluffy. I'm coming now. How's your head?" Ryder slipped on her boots, grabbed her weapons, and headed over to let Fluffy out. She knelt beside him and ruffled his head. "Have you got a hangover?" Ryder grinned. Her head was okay, thankfully. Last night with Javier had sobered her and the others right up. Everyone had fallen to sleep after they'd laid Javier to rest.

No one came to wake me for my turn to watch the house, she realized. Part of her wondered why, and another was grateful as hell because she'd taken such a beating yesterday. She was in a lot of pain from yesterday's fight, but she knew she could fight through it to free everyone. She would worry about recovery once it was all over. The adrenaline would keep her going for as long as she needed it to.

Ryder wrapped her arms around Fluffy and rested her head on his, and he nuzzled his nose under Ryder's chin. He was warm and…well, *fluffy.* "Your name suits you, you know." She winked, and for once Fluffy didn't growl back.

Ryder looked into Fluffy's big orange eyes. "Thank you

for waking me last night. It's nice to know you're always here, Leandro." She smiled, then got to her feet and opened the door.

Fluffy headed quickly toward the bathroom.

Ryder went straight down to the living room, where everyone was talking excitedly. "What's going on?" she asked Clint.

"It's Massimo. He's no longer an old man," Clint answered. "Look." He pointed at an unfamiliar man with black hair who wore the clothing Massimo had been wearing last night.

"Massimo?" Ryder asked, and the man turned around. Massimo was no longer hunched over. His spine was straight, his hair was black, peppered with a few gray strands, and he was radiantly handsome.

"Yes, Ryder?" Massimo's face was glowing.

Ryder was gobsmacked. "Shit, Massimo, apparently my blood is the good stuff!

Carter stood beside Ryder with his mouth open. He was as shocked as she was. Everyone in the room was staring at the man, trying to work out if it actually *was* Massimo.

Fluffy came back into the room and walked over to him. He sniffed Massimo and looked up at him, then went over to Ryder and sniffed the bandage around her forearm. Fluffy wagged his tail. He knew what they'd done.

Carter shrugged. "Well, if Fluffy approves, it must be Massimo,"

Fluffy growled at Carter. He still hated being called Fluffy, *especially* by Carter. Thanks to him, *everyone* called him Fluffy now.

Massimo smiled. "I'm an upgraded version. Massimo version 2.0, you could say."

Carter scratched his beard. "Oh, yeah, that's definitely Massimo."

Ryder grinned. "Damn! You said you were better-looking than Leandro, but I didn't know you weren't exaggerating." She turned to Fluffy. "Only joking." She winked. "Carter, looks like you've got some competition on your hands with *this* hot stud in the gang." Ryder loved the fact that Carter believed he was the best-looking guy here. It was so easy to wind him up about it.

Carter turned to Graham with an exaggerated expression of remorse. "Graham, you're dumped, mate. I'm sorry, there's a new man in my life now. No hard feelings, yeah?"

"Nothing is hard anymore," Graham deadpanned.

Carter winked at Massimo. "What do you say, good-looking?"

Massimo basked in the compliments. "You're making an old man blush."

Ryder chuckled. "You're not an old man anymore, Massimo. The upgrade looks good on you."

A few of the men looked at one another, Ryder knew what they were wondering—how the hell did it happen?

"How do *I* get an upgrade?" Carter asked.

Massimo pushed his hand through his black hair. You could tell he liked the feel of it, "You have to be a vampire." Massimo told him matter-of-factly.

A few of the men weren't too happy with the answer. *I can't have them thinking Massimo was sneaking around stealing people's blood.* "I gave Massimo some of my blood last night," Ryder told them. "We needed a strong vampire. A vegetarian vampire wasn't going to cut it." The men looked at her bandage. "I dripped my blood into a glass and gave it to Massimo. It was my idea. Massimo didn't want to do it, but I'm grateful he did."

The men nodded. Clearly, they were happy to have a strong vampire on their side as well.

"Is everyone ready to kick the shit out of some pricks?" Ryder said.

"*Fuck, yeah!*"

Leandro waited patiently for Ryder to wake up. He wanted to get out of his bedroom, but Ryder had closed the door before she went to bed, and because he was a wolf there was no way he could open it. Only now did he truly miss his thumbs. Also, his common sense. He'd been a wolf for one night and gotten hammered.

Still, he had good reason to want to drown his sorrows.

Last night while everyone was in the house eating, drinking, and reliving the day's events, Leandro had sneaked away to a quiet place to try to turn. He'd lain on the ground and thought hard about turning back into his human form, but the hours had ticked by and nothing had changed.

He'd surrendered to the idea that he wasn't going to be able to turn back to his human form. He had to accept that he was no longer a werewolf; he was only a wolf now. Part of him was okay with the idea. He did love being a wolf, but he also missed being able to speak with Massimo and Ryder. He had decided last night to drink away the pain of that, and this morning he was paying for it.

His head was pounding. That was no way to start off his first full day as a wolf. They were going into the fight of their lives. What had he been thinking?

That was the problem. He *hadn't* been thinking.

Leandro wanted to go to the bathroom. His bladder was full to bursting from all the alcohol he'd consumed.

He had a vague memory of licking Ryder's face. *Oh, Leandro! That's the most wolf-like thing I could have done. Where has my dignity gone?* He'd feared turning into a wolf would make him lose part of himself. He just wasn't expecting that part would be his sobriety. *That's it, I'm never drinking again! Why do people drink when they know they'll feel like shit the next day?* Leandro shook his head when he noticed Ryder getting to her feet. She must have heard what was going on in the living room.

Leandro sat at the door like a good pup and waited for Ryder to open the door. She looked down at him fondly. *Maybe she didn't remember last night? Please let her not remember.*

Then she said the words that let Leandro know she remembered last night just fine. "How's the head?"

Leandro wanted to curl up into a furry ball on the carpet and pretend like last night had never happened. He wanted to at least say he was sorry for his actions, that it was the drink, but he couldn't.

Instead, he lowered his head in shame, which was greeted by Ryder's hand pushing through his fur. *Oh, that's good. Don't stop,* Leandro thought. She was massaging the hangover right away.

Ryder lifted her hand off Leandro's head. *What part of "don't stop" did she not get?* She knelt beside Leandro and hugged him. He wanted to stay in her warm embrace forever.

Leandro's world almost ended when she let go of him and headed into the living room. He remembered the commotion he'd heard from the living room and followed her.

Before he could go into the living room, he had to get to the bathroom. *Dammit!* The bathroom door was closed. How the hell was he going to open it? Leandro heard singing through the door. It was an ABBA song, but it wasn't Massimo's voice. Leandro vaguely remembered Massimo playing it for his Merry Men and rolled his eyes. That was all Leandro needed—for everyone to enjoy ABBA as much as his Pops. Just the thought made his head hurt even more.

Then the handle turned, and Carter emerged. He was singing *Dancing Queen,* and he looked just like a queen— shiny clean and resplendent, with his bows in his freshly braided beard.

Carter looked down at Leandro, who hated the fact that Carter could look down at him. He had a puzzled look on his face, which was normal for him. "Oh, it's you, Fluffy. Do you need the bathroom?" Leandro growled in response. Carter grinned and swept an arm toward the bathroom. "Be my guest.'

Leandro pushed past Carter into the bathroom. This was *his* house, not Carter's. *He* was the guest here. Leandro went to close the door, but couldn't shut it all the way since there was a chance he'd get locked in. Carter peeked through the crack.

Leandro growled again. *Why was he watching?*

Leandro's bladder was too full for him to argue with Carter. He needed to piss. He turned to the toilet, and the *oh shit* moment came over him. He was a fucking wolf! He couldn't piss in a toilet. And of all people, it was Carter who had witnessed his fuck-up.

Carter started laughing and Leandro growled back, flashing his sharp teeth. "Easy, Fluffy. Go piss outside on a tree."

Leandro pushed past Carter. *What kind of animal does he think I am?*

"Come on, Fluffy, don't get all moody on me. You have to admit it was quite funny."

Leandro couldn't be bothered with Carter's smartass comments. He needed to get outside, or he was going to further humiliate himself by pissing on the floor. Leandro couldn't think of anything worse.

When Leandro passed through the living room, he caught a strange scent. It was his Pops, but he smelled different. Leandro sidetracked into the room, hoping he could hold his bladder a little longer. Massimo looked even younger than he had than when Leandro was a kid. His Pops had gone back in time. Leandro padded over to Massimo, completely and utterly shocked. What the hell had *happened* last night?

He remembered his dad speaking to him about something on the porch, but Leandro had been remembering how hot Ryder had looked shooting her bow. *That damn alcohol.* Leandro remembered agreeing to something, but not what. He now knew.

Leandro turned to look at Ryder, who had a bandage on her arm that he hadn't noticed. *She'd given Massimo her blood.* Looked like Leandro wasn't the only one who'd had a life-changing experience yesterday. They'd gone from father and son to wolf and vampire.

Massimo had finally given in to drinking human blood. *All those years of me having to force him into drinking rabbit's blood every morning, and as soon as a pretty girl walks in the house my dad is no longer a vegetarian? Bloody typical.*

The thought of drinking made Leandro remember that he needed to piss. He made a beeline for the exit and ran into the woods as far as he could so no one could see him.

He loved being able to run as fast as a speeding bullet, but he hated some of the other aspects of being a wolf.

Namely, pissing in public.

10

Just before sunrise, the group left Massimo's house and headed for Afana's bunker. Fluffy and Koda were at the front, leading them on the fastest route to the bunker. Fluffy knew a quicker route than the one Ryder had taken. This route took them around the mountains where Carter lived.

Ryder filled Massimo in on what had happened to Javier as they walked. "It's scary to think there's another way to turn Mad, isn't it? I thought getting bitten was bad enough."

"It is, really," he agreed. "How are we going to defend ourselves from something we know nothing about? I wonder if it is airborne after all." Massimo shook his head. "No. If it was, we would have all turned by now. It must be something that is already inside us, as I originally thought. I hope Afana has a computer and it's possible to link it to the outside world." Massimo's eyes widened at the thought, "Maybe there is someone out there who knows what's going on." Massimo nodded as he spoke. "There has to be. And we need to find that person before it takes any more good people."

Ryder smiled. "I hope you're right, and if you are, I'll help you find them."

Massimo's eyes crinkled with joy. "You are a sweetheart. Let me check with the others to find out how long it will be before we're there." He jogged over to Fluffy and Koda at the front of the group.

Massimo really did have a spring in his step. *My blood is damn good stuff!* Ryder thought and snickered. *Time to wind Carter up...* "Where's that lovely sweater Tightwad knitted for you?" Ryder asked, referring to the colorful sweater Tightwad had given him the night before. It looked like a fairy had farted on it, and it suited him perfectly since it matched the bows in his braids. Tightwad looked like he was wondering the same thing. He was wearing his colorful sweater, why not Carter?

"I didn't want to get blood splatters on it." Carter looked at Ryder as though it were obvious.

Tightwad had a look of horror on his face. "Oh, I hadn't thought of that. I should go back and change." Tightwad stroked his sweater fondly.

Carter smirked. "I have to say, Ryder, you're clearly dressed for a fight."

Ryder looked at her clothes—the ones she always wore—and back at Carter. "Go sit on a cactus." She laughed. Ever since she'd seen the cactus, Ryder had been waiting for an opportunity to make a joke involving the spiky plant.

Carter only looked confused; the joke was lost on him.

Next time, she would use it when Massimo was around. He would get it.

Ryder stroked Black Beauty. "Aren't you two riding together?" Ryder asked Carter and Graham. Graham had Black Beauty hitched to the cart, which was filled with extra weapons and other supplies.

"I fancied getting the blood flowing in my legs," Carter responded.

"What, instead of the blood being pumped to your dick?" Ryder snickered. Carter and Graham couldn't contain themselves and cracked up.

Carter's eyes widened. "Jeez, Ryder, you've got one dirty mouth."

Ryder grinned. "It comes with living in the bunker for years."

Massimo jogged back to the group. He didn't walk anymore; everything was a jog or a skip, like a school kid.

"Hey, Massimo, do you know Darth Vader?" Carter asked.

Ryder looked at Carter, puzzled. "Who's Darth Vader?"

Carter gasped. "Oh, he's Luke Skywalker's father."

"Spoiler!" Massimo shook his head. "You're not supposed to *tell* people what happened in the movie." He rolled his eyes, wondering how Carter could reveal such a big secret.

Carter was confused. "What? Why?"

Of course, he wouldn't know the rules since Massimo hadn't told him. He'd shared Carter's first movie, and hadn't told him the rules. "My bad. I should have told you. When you watch a movie, you don't tell others what happens, in case they want to watch it," Massimo explained. "Anyway, back to the question. I'm afraid I don't know Darth Vader or Luke Skywalker."

"How about lightsabers? Does Graham have one of those? That would be one killer weapon." Carter waved his axe around like it was a lightsaber, making the swooshing sound.

"We don't have any," Massimo admitted. "But it would be good if we did." Carter kept on with the swooshing noises as he swung his axe. Massimo smirked. "The Force is strong with you."

Carter's face lit up, and his eyes widened. "Really?"

Massimo nodded. "Really."

Koda raised his hand, and the group instantly stopped with their weapons in their hands. They were ready for anything. Koda pointed at the woods to the left that wrapped around the mountain.

They all waited for something to happen, then the leaves rustled and a red-eyed figure appeared. The Mad was covered in angry red sores, her clothes were ripped, and she had blood around her mouth.

Carter recognized the woman. "Rebecca, is that you?"

"If it was, it's not anymore," Byrant said. He was right. The Mad sprinted at the group.

"Kill shot," Ryder yelled. "Don't waste bullets!"

Byrant had his gun pointing at the woman. "Do it, Byrant," Everyone shouted at once. Carter had been working with him last night to build his confidence, which had taken a hit after he'd choked during the fight outside Graham's workshop.

"You've got this. Just pull the trigger," Carter told Byrant calmly.

Byrant squeezed his eyes shut and pulled the trigger.

Carter grinned and slapped Byrant on the back. "Looks like you really *are* the best gunslinger in town." Carter and the others were pleased that Byrant was back in form, since they needed him to be able to shoot at the bunker.

The Mad slumped to the ground. There was no need to two-tap; she wasn't going to come back to life after *that*.

Koda nodded. "Nice shot!" A few of the men agreed. There was a noticeable difference in Byrant. His confidence had begun to return.

Ryder was relieved since it meant they wouldn't have to worry about him freezing up and getting killed. They needed capable shooters on their side.

The group all looked down at Rebecca's body, except for Carter. He was looking in the direction Rebecca had appeared from.

The mountain settlement.

Carter's face was ashen with worry. "The kids," he breathed.

Ryder looked toward the settlement. She wouldn't leave the kids if there were Mad on the loose. They'd stand no chance. She hoped Terrier would wait for her, and wouldn't leave kids defenseless by getting killed.

"Change of plans," Ryder announced. "We need to check that Carter's settlement is okay first. Also, we may be able to get a few more people to help."

Everyone agreed without a fuss.

"Carter, we'll have to be quick. I don't want to lose too much daylight."

Carter nodded. "Thank you, Ryder. I'll take you by the

quickest route." He took off running with the group right beside him.

"Ryder," Graham shouted, and she turned around to see Graham on the cart. There was no way he could get up there with the cart and weapons. "I'll stay with Black Beauty," he called.

"Do you want someone else to stay with you?"

"Not when I have these." Graham swung his axes with a big grin on his face. "Hurry up, though. We don't want you getting lost."

He's right. My sense of direction sucks! Luckily, we have a wolf and a tracker in our gang, and they'll find me if I get lost. "Yell if you need us," she told him.

Ryder followed the others up the mountain. The ground was wet and mossy under her boots and she had to leap a number of fallen branches, but she caught up with the gang.

"Mad at three o'clock," Koda yelled. Everyone turned right to see a pair of glowing red eyes coming straight at the group.

"We got this one," Massimo said. He and Fluffy stood ready for the attack, and the rest of them kept running. It would take too much time if they hung around for each kill, and Ryder also knew that Massimo wanted to test his newly-regained strength. Part of Ryder wanted to see it, but that would happen soon enough.

Massimo's fangs protruded, and his eyes were aglow. He was in full vampire mode and felt stronger than he ever had before. The Mad was coming for them, but it had no idea that it was coming for Death. Leandro growled and made to spring at it, but Massimo stayed his son with a hand and moved forward to meet the Mad head on.

The Mad lunged at Massimo, but the vampire blocked its clumsy swipe and punched a hole through its skull. The Mad collapsed, falling off Massimo's fist with a wet pop. Massimo removed a clean handkerchief from his breast pocket and wiped his hands.

Fluffy gazed at Massimo in wonder.

"What?" Massimo asked. "I can fight, too."

The first things they heard when they reached the mountain settlement were the groans. Everyone had their weapons ready in a flash. Carter held up his hand, and the group slowly approached the sound.

It was coming from the cages with the infected parents. At least they hadn't escaped, although they looked worse than they had a day ago. They were more red sores on their exposed skin, and they were pissed. They reached through the bars try to grab the people as they passed.

Byrant had his gun out and was ready to shoot.

"Don't do it!" Carter ordered, getting between the Mad and Bryant's gun.

Willard looked at Carter, confused. "First he wants him to shoot, now he doesn't. Which is it?"

"They can't get out. I made sure of that," Carter assured them.

"Why are you keeping them?" Massimo asked when he

and Fluffy arrived. Massimo had blood spatters on his clothing, but Fluffy was his usual pristine white.

"Because they are the parents of some of the kids in the settlement. We need to see if their kids are all right," Carter reminded them as he pushed Byrant's gun down.

A child's scream rang out, and they all pelted in the direction it had come from. When they were almost at the settlement, the stench of rotting flesh hit them. There were two Mad on the ground. Their legs were gone, their flesh had been bitten away, and bones protruded through their exposed muscles. None of that stopped them from dragging themselves inch by inch toward the settlement.

Two wolves with blood around their mouths came sprinting down the hill and blocked their way. Both were white like Fluffy. The group looked at the wolves and then at Fluffy.

Ryder asked what they were all thinking. "Hey, Leandro, are you all related?"

Leandro walked up to the white wolves. They looked just like him, a male and a female version of himself. He chuffed at them, trying to find out what happened. They didn't respond, unless he could call licking their butts a response. *Disgusting.*

The female wolf stared at Leandro. He tried again, but it was like he was speaking to them in a different language. Maybe he was.

The male wolf headed over to a tree and pissed on it, right in front of everyone. *Does he not have any dignity?*

Carter laughed and pointed at the wolf. "See, Fluffy, *that's* how you have a piss."

Leandro cringed with embarrassment while Carter regaled the others with how he had caught Leandro trying to use the toilet. *I'm going to rip his vocal cords out one day to shut him up.*

Carter tried to break the tension between them and the wolves because they needed to get past them. Carter gingerly walked around them with his hands away from his axes to show the wolves that he had no intention of harming them.

They let him pass. It appeared as though they were only after the Mad, which was a good thing for the Merry Men. They all slowly walked around the wolves and the Mad, who were pulling themselves along the ground toward them like they wanted to bite down on their fresh flesh.

Massimo was the last person to walk around the Mad, and they moved quickly in his direction. Massimo stood his ground and snarled at them with his fangs on display. The Mad didn't even stop. They weren't scared of a vampire.

Which annoyed Massimo.

"I really don't have the effect on the Mad I was hoping for," Massimo complained.

One of the wolves snarled and darted at the Mad, then pulled on its leg tendons which stopped the Mad from getting any closer to Massimo. They were stopping the Mad. It looked gross, but Ryder was glad they were helping.

Leandro chuffed his thanks to the wolves. They looked

at him and then kept chowing down on the bloody tendons.

These animals are wild weirdos.

Leandro slowly walked away from the wolves and the Mad, following his pack.

When they reached the settlement, there was a fight going on between the mountain people and the Mad.

There were no kids there, so Ryder glanced around, terrified she'd see them on the ground. They weren't present, but there were dead Mad wherever she looked. There had already been one hell of a bloody fight, and it wasn't over.

Ryder glanced back. The wolves had followed them.

"Stop him," Maxwell, the leader of the mountain settlement, yelled as a Mad staggered away from the fight toward the watering hole where Ryder had washed her clothes.

"I've got him," Ryder called back. She nocked one of her cloth-wrapped arrows and dipped it in the alcohol. *Shit, I need someone to light it.* Before she could ask anyone, Carter was by her side. He took the flint and made a spark, and it was enough to light the arrow. Ryder aimed for the staggering Mad and let the arrow fly. It landed in the Mad's back and his dry, bloody shirt caught on fire.

The Mad dropped to the ground. He wasn't going anywhere now.

An oncoming Mad had his throat slashed before Ryder could shoot him and fell to the ground, cut down by

Maxwell. Louis and Andrew, who'd guarded her shack, joined them.

"Nice to see you again," Maxwell said as he fought alongside Ryder. "I wish it was under better circumstances."

"Me, too. Where are the kids?" Ryder asked. Carter leaned into the conversation as the three of them fought off the Mad.

"They are safe," Maxwell told them, and Carter left out a breath of relief.

A gurgle came from behind Ryder, and she turned to see the body of a man lifting itself up off the ground. His leg was in a weird position; it was broken and looked painful. His eyes were going red. He had the Madness.

Other bodies started to move. Some were even more beaten up than the man in front of Ryder. A few had limbs missing, but that wasn't going to stop them. They were all getting to their feet, and their eyes were all red.

Everyone around them was Mad.

The Mad on the ground weren't dead. "They weren't two-tapped," Ryder told Maxwell. "Headshots. Try to save your bullets when you can."

Then all hell broke loose. The Mad came at them, guns were fired, and bodies fell to the ground.

They were too close for Ryder to use her bow and arrows, so she used her knives instead, slashing any Mad that dared come near her. She wished she had Koda's spear. He was able to keep them at arm's length, whereas Ryder needed them to be closer for her to attack them. Koda stabbed the Mad with his spear, pulling it out and moving onto the next.

"Oh, fuck," Carter said abruptly.

Ryder glanced at him. He looked fine, and was fighting off Mad with his axe. Ryder scanned the area. Yes, they had a lot of Mad to kill, but there weren't any crazies running at them. They could handle this. They'd been through a lot worse.

"What?" Ryder asked during slashes.

"I've lost a bow," Carter said in a panic.

Ryder was confused since Carter wasn't an archer. "A bow?".

"Yeah. It was one of Jessica's favorites. She's going to be pissed." Carter was disappointed in himself.

Oh, a bow from his beard, Ryder realized. "She'll forgive you." Ryder smiled.

"I don't know. You know what girls are like," Carter said.

Ryder raised her eyebrow. She'd rarely been referred to as a girl. "What do you mean by that?" Ryder quizzed. *Time to have a bit of fun with Carter.*

Carter paused. He wasn't sure what to say and didn't want to end up at the end of Ryder's knife. "You know, touchy about their stuff."

"Hey, Vicky! Have you heard this? Apparently, us girls are touchy about our stuff," Ryder yelled over the noise.

A crunch came from the skull of Vicky's latest Mad as she swung. "Which dingbat said that?"

Ryder laughed. "I'll give you one guess."

Carter looked nervously at Ryder and Vicky, both women no one should fuck with.

"Carter," Vicky ground out.

Ryder smiled. "Yep, the one and only."

Carter gulped as they killed the next Mad.

The wolves went for the Mad, gripping their throats and not letting go until the Mad dropped to the ground. They quickly moved on to their next Mad.

Willard threw his knives into the oncoming Mad. Ryder knew he'd be useful at the bunker.

Fluffy went for a Mad who was heading toward Ryder and knocked him off his feet, then leaped onto the Mad and tossed him around like a ragdoll.

Dustin was getting up close and personal with the Mad, slashing and stabbing his way through them with the blades attached to his gloves.

Tightwad danced through the Mad, cleaving them in two with broad swings of his swords.

Vicky swung her shovel into a Mad's face, and there was a loud crunch as her teeth were shattered. That didn't stop the Madwoman; she came at Vicky with her toothless mouth open, her gums dripping with blood. The Mad didn't care. She just wanted to drink the untainted blood coursing through Vicky's veins and eat her fresh flesh.

The Mad had chosen the wrong woman to go after. Vicky swung the shovel again, and this time she made sure it landed properly. The Mad didn't stand a chance.

"Graham was right. I get a stronger whack when I twist my hips." Vicky thrust her hips from side to side and grinned, then slammed the shovel down on the Mad's neck.

Vicky went for another Mad who was on the ground. This one wasn't able to walk. It was pulling itself along the ground with its hands as it tried to get at Vicky. She slammed her shovel down, and this time blood sprayed up.

"Watch it! Oh, no, my sweater!" Tightwad exclaimed. He was standing close to the Mad and fighting off another one.

He looked upset as he stared down at his sweater, Ryder couldn't work out what was blood splatter and what was the random pattern.

Ryder had to hold in her amusement until she'd fought off the hungry Mad who was coming for her. The Mad looked like a crazy she-demon with her glowing red eyes and her arms stretched out. She was screeching as though she were trying to tell all of the other Mad that there was some tasty fresh blood for them.

Ryder went for a quick kill—just sliced the woman's throat and jumped out of the way. This was the quickest way, but it was also the messiest.

"Oh, *Ryder,*" Tightwad wailed. This time it wasn't only his sweater that had been sprayed with blood. Now his face was dripping with it as well.

Carter winked at Tightwad. "See, that's why I didn't want to wear it. You can have mine when we get back."

Tightwad swung his swords at a Mad. "Oh no…no…no." He was a little breathless from fighting. "I could never take back a gift. That's yours forever." Tightwad grinned at Carter and kept slaying Mad.

Carter now wished he'd worn the sweater.

11

Ryder and the Merry Men, working with the local people, had killed all the Mad. They made sure they weren't going to get back up again, and secured the mountain settlement.

They were all worn out from the fighting, except Massimo. *My blood really is super-amazing,* Ryder thought once again. It couldn't be *that* super, though, since she was worn out.

Once everyone got their breath back, Ryder spoke to Maxwell. "Where are the kids?"

"They are in a cave by the watering hole where you washed your clothes," Maxwell told Ryder.

Ryder knew that she couldn't let being tired take control of her today. "You guys wait here. Retrieve any weapons, because we'll be out of here in fifteen minutes." Ryder knew they had to get back on schedule.

Ryder, Carter, and a handful of people from the mountain settlement made their way to the watering hole.

"Sorry about bopping you over the head," Carter told Andrew. "And for tying you up," he added to Maxwell. "Natalie is still alive. I had to help."

Maxwell nodded. "We understand."

Andrew, on the other hand, didn't look like he understood. It actually seemed like he wanted Carter to go Mad so he could kill him without interference from Ryder and the others.

"What happened?" Carter asked Maxwell.

"It was crazy. All of a sudden people changed. We'd been out hunting, and everyone who was left in the settlement had gone Mad. We didn't have a chance. There were too many of them. I'm glad you turned up. I don't know *what* would have happened," Maxwell admitted.

Carter was annoyed that he hadn't been here when it all started, but he was glad he was here to finish it. "Holy shit, it *must* have been bad if you are glad I turned up. That has to be a fucking first," Carter said.

"It *was* that bad," Maxwell admitted. "The kids will be happy to see you." The men smiled at one another.

"Were any of them injured?" asked Carter, concerned.

Maxwell shook his head, "No, you trained them well. Better than most of the adults."

"Stop with all these compliments." Carter blushed under his beard and waved Maxwell away, then winked. "No, actually, go right ahead."

Maxwell shook his head. "You've been back for less than an hour, and you've already managed to wind me up." Maxwell smiled.

Carter laughed. "I said, no more compliments."

Maxwell nodded toward the cave. They were there.

Carter headed straight for the cave, and the other people hung back. "Aren't you coming?" he asked the group.

"No. I think just one of us would be better. We don't want to scare them," Maxwell told him, and the others nodded in agreement.

Carter took a quick glance at his clothing. He had blood splatters all over him, and his hands were even worse. He wiped his hands down his pants to clean them, since he didn't want to terrify the kids.

"Hey, guys. It's just me. Don't attack me," Carter called loudly enough for the kids to hear him. He slowly headed around the corner, to be confronted by a group of kids pointing knives at him.

He instantly put his hands up and surrendered. They froze for a moment, clearly not expecting Carter, then they ran at him hugging him. Carter was overwhelmed by their reactions.

If he hadn't been a big tough guy, he'd have a tear in his eye.

"Easy, guys. Are you trying to break me with these hugs? Maxwell told me you kicked some ass!" Carter told them proudly.

"We did! You should have seen us," Tommy burst out. "What are you doing here? Did you rescue everyone from the bunker?"

Carter had only been gone for a few days, but it felt like these kids had aged years since he'd been away.

"Not yet. We were on the way there, and I thought I'd pop in and say hi." Carter smiled. They didn't need to hear the real reason, even though they already knew.

"Is Ryder with you?" Tommy asked, looking past Carter. Tommy fired questions at Carter before he could give him a full answer.

"Yes."

Tommy grinned, wiggling his eyebrows. "Is she your girlfriend now?"

"No."

"Why? She's pretty." Tommy inquired, and the other kids nodded in agreement. "She is."

"*Carter and Ryder sitting in a tree...*" the kids sang, giggling.

"Guys, stop it. Come on, let's go see Ryder and my other friends. I'll introduce you to them."

A few of the kids looked wary. They were scared to leave the cave.

The kids ran to Maxwell and the others, but Jessica wasn't there. Carter panicked and called for her, and after a few moments, Jessica stepped out of the cave.

As soon as Jessica saw Carter, she folded her hands over her chest. "Carter, where's your yellow ribbon?"

Carter had been right. She was pissed. *Really* pissed.

"And your braids look a mess," Jessica chided. She walked over to Carter and began to fix them. She was also checking whether he'd lost any more.

"Nice to see you too," Carter said as he was getting told off.

Jessica stamped a tiny foot. "You know, you were only *borrowing* the ribbons. I thought I'd told you that." Ryder couldn't help but snigger and Jessica shot Ryder a look as if to say this wasn't a laughing matter, which made Ryder laugh even harder. They were both being told off by a six-year-old, and she looked damn cute doing it.

Jessica waited until Ryder had contained herself. "Come on, we'll have to get your braids sorted out." Her tiny hand slid into Carter's, and he was glad he'd cleaned them. She led him in the opposite direction from Maxwell and the others.

Ryder wondered where they were going, but didn't want to ask in case she got another scolding from Jessica.

"Jessica, do you want a shoulder ride?" Carter asked. Jessica took him up on the offer, and he lifted her up. After a few minutes, they came to a stone house, which was about the same size as Leandro's bedroom.

Carter put Jessica down, and they entered the tiny home. Ryder was shocked at what she saw. She thought nothing could be brighter than Tightwad's jumper, but it turned out she was wrong. The house was bulging at the seams with bright and colorful items. From ribbons to toys, it was a treasure chest of color.

"What *is* all this stuff?" Ryder asked. Her eyes were wandering around, trying to take it all in.

"It's the kids' toy box," Carter told her. Jessica headed straight for the ribbons.

This toy box made the toys Ryder and Terrier had made in the bunker look pathetic. This wasn't a toy box, it was a toy *house*. "Where did you get all this stuff?" Ryder asked.

"We collected it." Carter smiled and knelt for Jessica to fix is bows.

Jessica pointed a finger at Carter. "The rule is, we borrow things from the toy box, but we must bring them back," she said shaking her head at Carter. "You are always breaking the rules."

Carter shrugged and grinned. "You know me. Rule breaker."

Ryder couldn't help but think about Tightwad's face if he ever got in here. "Oh, my goodness. Tightwad is going to shit a rainbow when he sees all this!" Ryder held up brightly colored yarn.

Carter cracked up. "Shit a rainbow?"

Shit! Ryder placed her hand over her mouth. "Sorry, Jessica."

Ryder didn't need to be sorry. "Shit a *rainbow*." Carter repeated it several times, and each time he did Jessica laughed louder. In the end, the three of them were laughing so hard Ryder's ribs hurt.

Once Ryder, Carter, and Jessica had contained themselves, they headed back to the other kids. Carter looked a little better with his new neat bows.

Fluffy had come to walk by Ryder's side, even though he'd been told by the others to wait behind for her. Ryder was happy he hadn't listened, and so were the kids.

The kids looked around. "You didn't say Fluffy was here." They were joyful as they moved closer to Ryder.

Ryder remembered how she'd told them not to stroke him last time they were at the settlement. "You can stroke him if you want. He's a soft furball." Ryder smirked at Leandro, who just looked up at her and shook his head. Ryder smiled at the kids. "Take turns, though." She smiled again when the kids did as she'd requested.

"Fluffy, watch them while I talk with Maxwell and the others," Ryder told Fluffy.

The group moved away from the kids, who were still within sight but out of earshot so they couldn't hear what the adults were saying.

"What are you going to do now?" Ryder asked the group. There was only a handful of people from the settlement left, and they all turned to Maxwell for an answer.

"I can't take them back to the settlement after this. We'd need to do something with all the bodies." Maxwell shook his head. "And there aren't enough of us left to protect them if Afana's men came on a raid."

"There's a town called Pinewood. They also just had a Mad breakout, but I'm sure they'd take you in. I can speak to Massimo and see if you can stay at his house until he gets back." Ryder informed them.

"Would the kids be safe there?" he asked.

"They'd be safer there than here. To be honest, it's hard to tell if anywhere is safe, with these random cases of the Madness. The people in Pinewood are good folks, and they'd help look after the kids." That was one thing Ryder was sure of.

The kids made their way over to the group, "I want to go with you to the bunker," Tommy declared, and a few of the others agreed.

Carter knelt to be on their eye level. "It's no place for kids—" Carter began, but he was cut off.

Tommy's little face went red. "We fought off the Mad. We can fight off anyone else after that!" Tommy said with more grit than most adults. It made him look old beyond his years.

"I need you to protect Jessica and the others, and once we're done, we'll all be together again as one big happy dysfunctional family," Carter told him.

"You promise you'll come back for us?" Tommy asked.

"Of course! Where else would I go?" Carter ruffled Tommy's hair. "Let's go. Sooner I go, the sooner I can come back."

Afana dropped through the hole from Level One to Level Two, where the advisors and their families lived.

"Help us, Afana. Please," a woman sobbed. Her infant son was in her arms as she ran toward Afana with one of the infected chasing her. This was new for him. Normally people hid in fear, and children would cry. These emotions were new for Afana, and he didn't care too much for them. He just shrugged, and the woman looked at him in horror. *That's better,* he thought.

She ran past him, and the infected got closer to Afana. With a mighty swing, he punched the infected, who flew across the bunker and crashed into the wall.

"Thank you. Thank you," the woman sobbed. He hadn't done it for her, but for himself.

Afana headed for the Mad body that was on the floor, picked it up, and twisted its head until it crunched. That motherfucker wasn't going to get up again.

He took a glance around. Apparently one of the advisors had the disease. Screams came from down one of the tunnels off the social area, then more women and kids ran toward Afana and past him. Some of them stopped suddenly, shocked when they saw the vampire, then kept running.

Thuds came from the back of the screaming pack when more were pulled to the ground.

Through a gap of the fleeing crowd, Afana saw a child on all fours bounding like a wild animal, still wearing her nightgown. The snarling child had blood on her face and mindless, glowing red eyes. She pounced on a woman's back and sank her teeth into her neck, then thrashed her head to tear a chunk loose. Her hair swung violently as she pulled the woman's flesh free.

Other infected saw that there was a new meal on the floor for them, and they surrounded the body and began to feed on it.

The uninfected were behind Afana, trying to get as far away from the danger as possible.

I'm the monster down here, not these little shits. Afana marched over to the feeding Mad and pulled them off the latest victim.

They thrashed around, trying to latch onto Afana, and an infected woman leaped on Afana's back. She tried to bite him. Afana's skin was tough, but the infected was relentless. Her teeth sank into Afana's back, and he gripped her by her hair and dragged her off him. "You bitch!" He snapped her neck, then ripped the woman in two. He was furious that he'd been bitten, Advisor Robert's blood samples had shown that Afana could get the disease if he were infected with a lot of the virus. *One bite couldn't transmit a lot of the virus. I just won't get bitten again,* Afana thought.

Another infected ran at him, but this time he wasn't going to let the fucker bite him.

He pushed his hands into the infected man's mouth and pulled. His jaw came away with a sickening rip.

A man ran up to Afana. "Thank you, Afana! You saved me!"

Fuck this! He grabbed the man and snapped his neck, then threw his body across the bunker. "No more fucking thank yous!"

Others went for Afana, and he swung his oversized fists at them. Bodies flew across the bunker and crashed against the walls. He felt a sharp pain in his thigh; an infected had wrapped his arms around Afana's thigh and dug his teeth in. The vampire pulled the man off him and crushed his skull, but the damage had already been done.

Afana stopped when there was no one left to kill, feeling a little weak from the fighting. He wondered if it was from the bites. With all the carnage around him, he just wanted to drink blood to repair the damage.

He had to get to Level Six and feed on the non-infected.

Everyone on Level Six was in shock that they'd seen Evelyn taking chunks out of people and that she'd been able to knock Terrier to the floor. He was built like a brick wall, and Evelyn was a petite as they came. How could someone so small be so strong? What did the Madness do to her, and how had she been infected?

Some of the men who had been bitten were crying out in pain, and they had their hands wrapped around their gaping wounds as they tried to stem the blood flow. Blood was oozing through their fingers, and their faces were as white as snow. Evelyn had bitten down on the main arteries in the neck. They needed to stop the blood. If they didn't, they'd be dead soon.

General Murray looked at all the blood. "Get some sheets, blankets, and anything else we can use to stop the bleeding."

The women looked at him for a moment. Most of them were done following orders from the generals, but some ran off since the men Evelyn had bitten were their boyfriends.

"Ladies, you heard the man. Get help!" Mama Lou yelled, looking at them in disgust. The women quickly followed Mama Lou's orders. She knew why the women were hesitant, but she'd brought them up better than that. They needed to help the injured. She would speak with them later about that. They couldn't let the years of their captivity control them once they got out of here.

Shelly returned with a white sheet and hastily bundled it into Murray's hands.

"Thank you."

Shelly nodded. "Please help him." She knelt beside the man, who was her boyfriend.

"I'll do what I can." Murray ripped the sheet up, and he pushed a strip against his open wound. "Place your hand here," he told Shelly, and she quickly followed his order.

"Lift your hand." She did as he instructed, and Murray wrapped the makeshift bandage all the way around the man's neck. "This will help stop the bleeding," Murray told Shelly.

"Thank you! Thank you," Shelly repeated.

General Murray rested his hand on Shelly's shoulder to comfort her. He looked into her eyes and felt her pain. He only wished he'd been able to help her boyfriend earlier.

General Murray moved to work on the next person, but Terrier and Peter were already working on him. He looked around, and everyone was helping someone. This was how the bunker should have been from Day One. Afana had destroyed all of their lives.

Once the men had been bandaged, Terrier hurried over to Natalie. "Had Evelyn been bitten? Was one of the kids infected?"

"No, she wasn't bitten, and she didn't bite any of the kids." Natalie's breath hitched as she tried to hold in her tears. One of her closest friends had caught the disease and was now dead.

"Are you sure?" Terrier pressed.

The people around them who were listening began to feel uncomfortable in their own skin, as if at any moment they could succumb to the infection.

Natalie nodded. "I'm sure. She was behaving normally, then Chloe told me that Evelyn was acting …weird. She kept stopping the story, and the kids were getting annoyed." Natalie paused as she looked down at Evelyn's body. "She was just reading a story a few moments ago." Terrier rubbed her back to comfort her, and Natalie looked up at Terrier. "I remembered you telling me to look out for people behaving differently…and she was. When I went to check on her…" Natalie raised her hand to her mouth, "her eyes were glowing red, and her mouth was bleeding."

General Murray took one of the sheets and gently draped it over Evelyn's body.

"Natalie, Jasmine, can you take the kids to their room?" Mama Lou asked.

Natalie led the kids away.

"How does this damn virus spread?" Mama Lou asked, and others nodded. People spoke among themselves, but no one had the answer.

General Murray wiped the blood from the injured down his pants. "Martin was bitten by an infected, and Advisor George felt that he was going to change. It seems like there are two ways to get the disease."

Their eyes rested on the ones who had been bitten, and they had fear in their eyes. Originally, they were afraid of dying because of the loss of blood, and now they were terrified that they were infected.

The level fell quiet.

The wolves had followed Leandro when he walked with the others in the direction of Graham's cart. Leandro had tried to talk with them again but had once more gotten no response. He'd given up.

Then he noticed they'd stopped, and he turned toward them. Massimo was by Leandro's side, and he paused as well. The others hadn't noticed and kept walking toward Graham's cart.

Massimo looked down at Leandro. "I understand if you want to go with them and be part of a pack."

I don't understand. Why would I want to be with those pissing-in-public, butt-licking wolves? Leandro wondered.

Leandro stared up at his dad and shook his head. This upgraded version of his Pops didn't seem to be the brightest. Massimo and his Merry Men were Leandro's pack.

The Were headed back down the mountain, and Massimo followed with a smile on his face. He rubbed the top of Leandro's head. "Glad you decided to stay."

Leandro looked back at the two white wolves, who were watching him as he left. He wondered if they were his parents, once werewolves who were now trapped as wolves just like him. The difference between them and him was that they had lost who they were on the inside. Their humanity.

Leandro had no intentions of doing that. He'd always be Leandro, even if everyone called him Fluffy. He was Massimo's son Leandro, and proud of it. So what if he was stuck on four feet? Now he was like Massimo, an upgraded version of himself.

Leandro liked that idea.

———

The original group and the people from the mountain settlement reached Graham and Black Beauty, and the kids occupied themselves by petting Black Beauty while the adults talked.

Massimo had told the adults from the mountain settlement where his home was, and that they could treat it as their own. When he returned, he'd help them get settled into new homes.

Massimo truly was a good guy. Ryder smiled at Massimo once he'd finished.

Carter was close to tears. "Thank you, Massimo."

No smart-ass comments, just a nice thank you, Ryder thought.

Massimo beamed. "You're welcome, Carter and my new friends. The house is going to be lovely and full of life with all of you in it. We'd best be going. Soon Pinewood will be full of people."

Ryder could see that Massimo was happy with that idea, which pleased Ryder. She'd hoped that once she'd gotten everyone out of the bunker, they'd be able to live in Pinewood.

Everyone said goodbye to the kids and prepared to get back on the road. The kids gave Carter and Ryder hugs. Ryder was looking forward to seeing the kids in the bunker, and soon she would.

"Keep them safe," Carter told Maxwell.

Maxwell patted Carter's back. "They will."

"*They* will?" Carter said, raising his eyebrow.

"Yes. We've decided to help you," Maxwell told him. Louis and Andrew nodded. "Those are *our* people that he's holding, and they've been there too long," Maxwell admitted.

Carter was silent for once as his mind went to Natalie and all the years she'd been living in the bunker. Horrible thoughts passed through his mind, and he could feel his blood boiling. He needed to stop thinking about it and block it out like he'd done all his life.

Ewoks sprang into his mind, much to his relief, and he looked at the woody landscape. *I'll find you if you're out there, and you can be my furry buddies.*

Maxwell's voice snapped Carter out of his Ewok daydream. "We'll need some weapons since we've given ours to them," Maxwell said, pointing to the adults leading the kids in the direction of Massimo's home.

Graham was ready. "Did someone say they needed

some weapons?" Graham produced a handful of long knives and grinned at them all.

"We've got weapons. Thank you for joining us," Ryder told them.

Maxwell shook his head. "We should have done this a long time ago."

Ryder disagreed. "You would have died."

"Here she goes again with her uplifting pep talk." Carter tugged on a braid. When he let go, Ryder noticed that there were new braids with pink bows. Jessica was quick at cleaning Carter up.

Ryder rolled her eyes at Carter. "By that, I mean because you didn't have the Merry Men with you."

"I think she's quite good at pep talks," Maxwell told Carter.

"She learned from the best," Carter bragged.

"Carter's taking credit again? Go deep-throat a cactus." Ryder laughed, and Massimo was quick to laugh alongside her.

"Deep-throat a cactus! I love it! That's one of your best," Massimo managed between gales of laughter.

Ryder took a bow. "Why, thank you, kind sir. I've wanted to use that one for a while, but the right moment hadn't come up." The two laughed together and the others watched on in bemusement, missing their inside joke.

"What is it with you and cactus? I have no clue what you're talking about!" Carter was still confused, which pleased Ryder even more.

"I'll show you when we get back to Massimo's house since you and it have a lot in common," Ryder informed Carter.

Carter stood proudly. "We do? Are we both handsome?"

"You're both little pricks." That was it. The two couldn't contain themselves. Massimo and Ryder were both crying with laughter.

Graham looked down at them from the cart. He passed the weapons down, shaking his head.

Ryder put her hand over her mouth to stop her laughter and asked, "Graham, have you got another one of those badass spears?"

"Since you asked so nicely, I do." Graham reached into the cart and pulled out a wooden spear like Koda's.

"Sweet!" Ryder banged the end of the spear on the ground, and knives extended from the bottom when she pressed a button. "Has anyone told you you're one badass blacksmith?"

Graham grinned. "They have now."

Carter was looking around at the forest. Everyone did the same every so often since they were worried a Mad might spring out in front of them.

Carter seemed to be scanning the area more than the others, and Massimo had noticed. "I can't smell any of them," Massimo said.

"They smell?"

Carter looked at Massimo, a little confused. "They smell?"

"Yes, like rotten eggs."

"Ewoks smell like rotten eggs?"

"Ewoks?" Massimo laughed. "How many Star Wars movies did you watch last night?"

"Not enough. I know they are shy, but in all my years

living in the mountain settlement, I've never seen an Ewok. Have you?" Carter asked Massimo in wonder.

Massimo pondered his answer. "I've seen a couple over the years." It was too delicious not to play along.

"You have?" Carter was excited and glanced around again. "I hope I see them."

Massimo grinned like a little kid.

Tightwad was brushing his sweater, trying to get the blood off it. He was really upset. He took out his flask and knocked back a drink, then wiped his lips. Ryder felt bad for Tightwad. She should have told him not to wear his favorite clothing.

"Shit rainbows!" Ryder blurted. Everyone looked at Ryder like she'd gone crazy.

Ryder giggled. "Up at the mountain settlement, they have a house filled with all different cool stuff and colorful yarn," she informed Tightwad.

Tightwad's face lit up. "Yarn?"

Ryder nodded. "There was a lot there." *Shit, Jessica had said they could only borrow it. She's going to be pissed at me now.*

Carter's eyes bulged when she said that, then he grinned. "As long as he's borrowing it, it's fine."

"Dick!" she said, shaking her head and smiling.

"I can?" Tightwad asked nervously.

"You can," Carter agreed.

Tightwad bounced with excitement. "I'm going to make one for everyone! All the Merry Men can have a new sweater!"

Oh, shit, I put my foot in it now! Ryder thought.

Carter started laughing when he'd worked out what was going through Ryder's mind.

Ryder thought it was time to change the subject. "Right, we're going to run to make up for lost time."

The others didn't look impressed by the idea of a run.

"Come on, you chickenshits, let's race! Are you afraid to be beaten by a girl?" Ryder laughed as she ran ahead of them, Fluffy by her side.

The men looked at one another.

"Fuck that." Carter quickly caught up with Ryder.

Graham jumped on Black Beauty, "Laters, chickenshits." He laughed and rode away from the others.

Massimo turned to run. "You're going to lose to a girl *and* a two-hundred-plus-years-old man? Peace out, chickenshits."

The remaining men and Vicky looked at one another. None of them wanted to be last, so they took off after the others.

Everyone had slowed from a run to a quick walk. They were still a fair distance from Afana's bunker, and they didn't want to get worn out before the fight had actually begun.

The path they walked along was wet and muddy, but passable. Luckily the trees weren't too thick, and the horses could continue with them. On the horizon, Ryder could see the thick woods in front of Afana's bunker.

Ryder walked between Massimo and Fluffy. "Massimo, will you tell me now what happened on the World's Worst Day Ever?" Ryder had asked Massimo when they were at his home, and Massimo had promised to tell her.

Massimo nodded somberly. "I suppose we have the time now." He smiled, but the smile didn't reach his eyes. "The world was very different before the World's Worst Day Ever. People lived in homes very much like mine in towns like Pinewood. Pinewood is very small compared to the cities, where thousands upon thousands of people lived together."

Ryder looked at Massimo. "What, like the bunker?" Ryder was thinking that the world before WWDE was better than today.

Massimo quickly shook his head. "Oh. Oh, no. People were allowed to travel freely around the world, and could live where ever they wanted."

Ryder's eyes lit up. "Nice! Like life *before* the bunker."

Massimo let out a little laugh. "Yes. Some city dwellers felt like they were living in a bunker, though. They were living in very, *very* tiny apartments, with not enough room to swing a cat. In some city apartments, they could stretch out their arms and each hand could touch a wall. They were very small." Massimo stretched his arms out to illustrate.

Ryder was a little confused. "That doesn't sound like much fun."

Massimo was enjoying this conversation. "In New York City, there were over eight million people all living on top of each other." Massimo smiled fondly. "New York was a fun city. I've got a lot of good memories."

Ryder left him to his memories for a moment.

Massimo shook himself. "Sorry, where was I? Oh, yes—WWDE. It is thought that the World's Worst Day Ever was started in China by a grieving father with access to a deadly computer virus."

Ryder didn't have a clue what Massimo was talking about, and by the look on her face, Massimo knew it. "How can a computer virus be deadly?" She knew next to nothing about computers, other than that Afana used them to run the bunker and watch the people on the levels.

"Back in the day, computers ran the world," Massimo explained. "The virus made everything the computers ran fail, and without them, civilization failed."

Ryder raised her eyebrow, "A bit like the Madness, then?"

Massimo's eyes widened at Ryder's perception. "Actually, you may be right. At first, the virus spread using the social media networks. People all over the world spread the code unwittingly through their online communications."

Ryder remembered that Massimo had mentioned something similar earlier. "Like on Facebook?"

"Yes, like Facebook. Since all the computers talked to one another, the virus spread quickly. But computers weren't there just so people could talk to one another. They also powered everything: medical equipment, utilities, water, nuclear bombs. They all ran on computers. The virus spread fast and far, and before they knew it, it was too late." He shook his head soberly.

"How do you know all this stuff?" Ryder quizzed.

Massimo sighed and kicked a stone into the foliage. "I worked with computers; it was my job. We worked out what was going on before everyone else, but it was too late. The virus had already spread."

Ryder came back to her insight about the Madness outbreak. "This virus sounds like the Madness, which is spreading fast. How do you think people are getting it without being bitten?"

Massimo thought about Javier; how he hadn't been

bitten, yet had become Mad. "It's like a new piece of code has been added? A switch was flicked, and it turned on the Madness."

Ryder frowned at Massimo. "Where did the switch come from? Do you think it was inside us all along?" It felt good to put her suspicions into words.

Massimo stared at Ryder and placed his finger on his lips as he thought. "Ryder, you may be onto something. There are nanocytes inside me. They are what made me into a vampire. Maybe those who turn Mad have nanocytes in *them*."

Ryder waved her hands at Massimo. "Nanocytes?" Ryder was more than confused by the words.

Massimo pressed his thumb and forefinger together. "Nanocytes are tiny computers which are in my bloodstream. Leandro's too, although he has a different kind than I do. Possibly, just possibly, others have nanocytes as well? What if someone was screwing around with them, and the result was the Madness?" Massimo wandered in thought for a moment while he considered the implications. "Bethany Anne would never have allowed anyone to play God like that."

Ryder gave him a quizzical look. "Bethany Anne?"

Massimo shook his head. "A tale, or rather many tales, for another day, my dear."

Ryder shrugged and let it pass. "I wonder if there is a way to switch the Madness off?"

"I honestly don't know," Massimo admitted. "Does Afana have much modern equipment in the bunker?"

Ryder nodded. "On Level One, there is loads of stuff

that looks like it's from the future, but really it's from the past. The advisors use the equipment to run the bunker."

Massimo nodded, "I'll take a look at it once we've taken over the bunker." He grinned.

Massimo looked like there was no doubt in his mind that they would overthrow the bunker. Ryder liked his confidence.

Ryder took a deep breath. They were near the tree line in front of the bunker. Only a few days ago Ryder had run for her life through these woods, and Fluffy had protected her from the tiger and then dragged her out of the stream.

She looked down at Fluffy, who'd walked alongside her for most of the journey. Ryder was grateful for the company. She stroked Fluffy's back. "Thank you for protecting me." Fluffy looked up at her and chuffed. He really was a handsome wolf, but she knew Leandro was still in there.

Every so often, Fluffy would sniff the air. Ryder thought he was checking for the Mad or people from the bunker.

Fluffy was always protecting her.

She wondered how his hangover was, then laughed when she remembered Massimo telling her that he didn't drink and had never been drunk. She kind of understood why he had decided to do that as a wolf. Ryder had been drunk more times than she could remember; sometimes out of choice, other times not. Thinking about drinking made Ryder thirsty, so she took a sip of water and then drank some of Massimo's hard alcohol. That way she could have a clear head, since one balanced the other.

She had noticed when they were leaving Massimo's

house that Tightwad also had two water flasks. She guessed that his contained the same as hers, and she hoped he was planning to balance his fluid intake like she was.

Tightwad's skill with the swords when he fought against the Mad had taken Ryder by surprise. Graham had definitely given him the right weapon. Ryder was looking forward to the using new spear he'd given her and was excited about serving some Justice with it. It was going to go right through Afana's men's motherfucking hearts. It was what they deserved after keeping her and the others captive, but then again, those fuckers probably didn't *have* hearts. She'd stab them in that spot anyway, but instead of blood on the blade tip, she was expecting to see black slime. These men were going to go straight to Hell, and Ryder was going to send them there.

Graham drew the cart to a stop. "The trees are too thick here. We'll have to carry our weapons from this point, and leave Black Beauty tied up with the cart." Graham lifted the blanket up to reveal the weapons—and little Tommy.

Everyone was surprised when the mountain kid Ryder, Carter, and Fluffy had protected from the bear sat up from under the blanket and gave everyone a nervous smile. "Um, hi?"

"What are you doing here?" Carter sounded like a disapproving parent.

Tommy's smile quickly faded. He knew he was in trouble. "I can help," he pleaded.

Carter looked at the sky in the hope that a higher power would give him strength, or at least an idea what to do with the kid. "This isn't a safe place for you," Carter told him, shaking his head.

Tommy thought quickly. "I can help lay traps. You know I'm the best at that," Tommy said in a hurry, and Carter nodded. "See?"

"Not so fast," Carter said sternly, acting all grown up. It was a funny sight to see. "You can stay with Black Beauty and create traps around her and you," Carter told him.

"But—" Tommy began.

Carter cut him off. "No buts." He shook his finger at Tommy, who pressed his lips together as he tried to bite his tongue. "Hop on down so everyone can get their weapons."

Tommy did as Carter instructed, and everyone leaned into the cart and collected their weapons. Ryder got extra knives and strapped them around her legs. She added more arrows to the quiver on her back. She could use the alcohol Massimo had given her to make them flame. She had a flint and steel in her pocket. Finally, she retrieved her new spear. It was very lightweight, which was perfect because she could handle it with ease.

Ryder was ready. She looked around at the rest, and they were ready too.

"We need to tread carefully through the forest. Tigers, bears, wolves, and other animals live in there. There will also be hunters, who will be hunting the animals and anything else that crosses them. Which includes us." Ryder told the group.

"Oh, my!" Massimo chuckled at his own joke, but, as usual, none of the others got the reference.

"They can try to hunt us." Graham spun his axes. "My two friends are looking forward to meeting them." He grinned at them all.

Ryder didn't want any of them getting injured, or

worse, killed. "Don't underestimate them. For their whole lives, all they have done is hunt, and some of them are very good at it."

Carter turned to Tommy. "Don't leave this cart. Are you listening?" Carter spoke sternly.

Tommy lowered his head. "I'm listening." Tommy looked and sounded disappointed.

The Merry Men made their way toward the bunker. They were ready for anything. They would be the first to fire and shoot to kill, Ryder was sure. The Merry Men were going to take control of the bunker, free every innocent person, and make those who had trapped them there pay for it.

That was Ryder's promise, and apparently everyone else's.

The forest in front of Afana's bunker was quiet, and Ryder didn't like it—not one bit. It was too quiet, and too easy. There were no hunters or animals; the place was devoid of anything living. Ryder had never seen it like this. Something must be happening. There was no way that Afana could know they were coming since she'd killed the hunters who came after her. There was no one else. How could he possibly know?

Ryder raised her hand, and the group stopped. They'd reached the bunker, but there was no one guarding the entrance.

What the fuck?

A rustle came from the left, and everyone turned to it with their weapons ready. "Don't shoot, it's only me," Tommy called as he came into view.

Ryder raised her eyebrow. "Tommy."

Everyone muttered, and the kid looked sorry.

Carter was furious. "Get back to the cart," he snapped in his most grown-up voice.

Tommy started to speak. "But—"

Carter cut him off before he could say any more. "I'll shoot you in the butt if you don't make a run for it!"

Tommy looked at Carter in fear, since Carter was a good shot. Tommy legged it back to the cart.

"That kid." Carter shook his head.

"He reminds me of you," Ryder replied.

"What, cute?" Carter grinned. This wasn't the time for a back-and-forth game. They had a fight to win.

Ryder turned to the others. "Something is happening. There were no men or animals in the forest, and now there is no one guarding the bunker. And then there is the smell of rotten flesh. I don't think Afana knows that we're here. I think he's fighting a battle in the bunker." Ryder was concerned. Was Terrier in danger, or was he the one who had caused this? Had he already escaped? The questions whizzed through Ryder's mind. Was she too late?

"Do you want to go ahead?" Massimo asked. "What if there are Mad down there?"

"If that's the case, we can use it to our advantage. The generals will hopefully be distracted by the Mad, and we can attack them while they're not paying attention," Ryder explained.

Carter was anxious to get inside the bunker. "Hopefully. Let's get inside and see."

Ryder felt the adrenaline running through her body. She was ready to get back into the bunker and free Terrier and the others.

Ryder pulled on the handle and the heavy metal door actually opened. She hadn't been expecting that. She'd thought that they would have had to use the explosives Graham had brought with him. Ryder turned to Graham and saw the disappointment on his face and the explosives in his hand. She shook her head, and he unwillingly put them back into his backpack.

She wondered why the doors were open and had no guard, but she'd happily accept the invitation. With the help of the others, she pulled open the door. For each millimeter they opened the door, Ryder's heart rate increased. She'd be lying if she said she wasn't shitting herself, but this wasn't about her feelings. It was about her friends.

When they'd opened the door enough for them to enter, the place was eerily quiet. This was normal for Level One. The bunker was soundproofed so Afana couldn't hear the noise from the lower levels. The lower levels were the noisiest since they were the fullest.

Fluffy was right by Ryder's side as she walked into the bunker. This was the calm before the storm.

In front of them was where the advisors worked, behind a glass wall with a door that led to the outside. Over the years a few had tried to escape when the door guards weren't looking, but they never got far. Normally the daylight was a shock to their system. They'd gaze at the blue sky, which they'd only seen glimpses of from their work area.

Those who were captured ended up in the lab next to the work area and would become the next experimental body for their co-workers. That alone was enough to prevent most of them from trying to leave.

Ryder led the group along the wall out of the eyesight of the advisors, who were at that moment looking down through the glass floor.

Ryder waved Massimo to the front of the group, then pointed at the advisors' stations. "You need to turn the cameras off from there and open the doors," Ryder informed Massimo. She didn't know how or where, only that he could turn them off from there. All she remembered was Advisor George bitching about resetting the cameras from Level One when he came to the lower levels to fix the cameras she'd broken.

"I've got this. Come on, Leandro," Massimo said to Fluffy. Massimo didn't see the wolf, just his son. Just like Ryder.

"Good luck," Ryder said.

"Luck? A vampire and a wolf don't need luck. Those we go after do." Massimo grinned, enjoying his new strength. "Call us if you need us. We can hear you wherever you are." Massimo nodded reassuringly. With that, the father and son, vampire and werewolf, took off toward the advisors' stations. They ran along the wall, hiding in the shadows.

The plan was for them to wait till Massimo had turned off the cameras, so the advisors wouldn't be able to alert the bunker that they were here. Part of Ryder wondered if they still needed to follow that plan. She had to find out if there were Mad on the loose in the bunker.

Ryder paused. "Wait here."

Ryder edged forward. She had to get to the glass floor so could see down to Level Six.

Ryder was shocked when she looked down. The glass floors were smeared with blood, and there were piles of bodies. She gasped in horror and leaned back, bumping into something. She swung around, but it was just Carter.

"Carter!" Ryder hissed through gritted teeth.

He wasn't paying her any attention; he was looking down through the levels. "This place is huge. Where is Natalie?"

"At the bottom, on Level Six," Ryder informed him. He was right. The place *was* huge.

Carter squinted to get a better look down to the lowest level, but the blood-covered glass floors made it impossible.

The others had joined them as well.

So much for them following orders, Ryder thought.

There was no one around to see them, so they didn't need to hide. *Oh, shit, the cameras! How could she have been so dumb?* The cameras were pointing right at them, so she quickly looked at the advisors. They weren't looking at her. Ryder couldn't see the computers because the advisors were blocking the screens. Their eyes were still locked on the glass floor, watching what was happening beneath them, which meant that the cameras weren't working. George hadn't fixed them yet, and no wonder, with everything going on.

That meant that Massimo and Leandro didn't need to turn off the cameras.

"Come back," Ryder whispered.

Massimo and Leandro turned to face Ryder. They'd heard her whisper, but it was too late.

They were already in front of the glass wall, and the advisors had seen them.

Massimo turned away from Ryder. As he did, his fangs protruded out of his gums, and his eyes glowed red. The advisors who had spotted Massimo were staring at him in horror, and the others quickly followed suit.

He pushed open the door, which wasn't locked. There were squeaks from the Advisors' chairs as they quickly got to their feet and backed away from Massimo and Leandro. This wasn't quite the fight the two had expected. The advisors' faces were as white as their lab coats as they backed away from Massimo and Leandro.

"How do we turn off the cameras?" Massimo used his vampiric voice, and Leandro let out a growl for good measure. When the advisors shook their heads, he sighed. This would mean a fight. He moved in front of them. "Tell me!"

One of the advisors rushed at Massimo with something metal in his raised hand. Massimo wasn't going to take any shit from this lab guy. They needed answers and quickly. Massimo twisted the man's head off like a daisy, then dropped it to the floor. The man's body followed it.

"Tell me, or that will happen to you!" Massimo wasn't messing around.

"They… They…*are* down," an advisor spluttered, pointing to the blank monitors.

"Down?" Massimo repeated.

The man was right. The monitors weren't showing anything.

"Well, that was easy." Massimo looked at Leandro, who was standing by his side. Leandro looked up at his dad blankly and shook his head.

The advisors looked on with wonder and fear. The vampire was speaking to a wolf?

Leandro walked over to the door and nudged it, then glanced back at Massimo.

"What?" Massimo exclaimed, raising his hands. Leandro growled in frustration. He tilted his head to the door and then at the advisors.

Massimo pushed his hand through his silky hair, then did it again. He liked the way his hair now felt; so much thicker. "Do you want me to take them outside?" Massimo asked.

That was greeted with a growl.

Ryder was stood in the doorway now along with the others. "Are the cameras off?" she asked.

Massimo nodded. "Yes. Apparently, they were already off."

"And the doors. Are they open?"

"Oh, *that's* what Leandro was trying to tell me. I'm losing my marbles in my old age." Massimo grinned, a little embarrassed. He only had two tasks, and he'd forgotten one of them. He put it down to adrenaline messing with his brain cells.

Ryder marched over to the head advisor. "Advisor Robert, why are they open?" She narrowed her eyes, wondering why Robert was here. He was always by Afana's side. He was his right-hand slimeball. She grabbed him by the lapels of his lab coat and shook him roughly. "How come?"

"Because Afana opened them. He's about to clear the trash out of Level Six," he replied with a menacing grin on his face.

Ryder was confused. "Why?"

The slimeball's smile grew. "To get to Terrier and the other traitors. Then he's coming after *you*." Advisor Robert laughed happily.

Ryder was right up in Advisor Robert's face now. "Not if I find him first."

15

"Well, *that* was easier than I thought it would be," Ryder remarked. "Let's get them in the lab in case there is another way for them to alert Afana that we are here."

Massimo nodded in agreement. "Good idea."

He pushed open the door to the lab. "Holy snot balls." Ryder almost gagged when she spotted Knuckles strapped to a bed and a pile of what looked like Tank on the floor. His body was bloated like Afana's, and his eyes were like Ivan's. He appeared to be a mix of Mad and vampire, which wasn't a good look. Knuckles didn't look any better. He was staring into the distance rather than looking at them. It was like he hadn't seen them.

"That's Tank and Knuckles. Those two usually guard the bunker. Looks like Afana had other plans for them today." Ryder turned to Advisor Robert. "Is this your handiwork?"

"It was for science," Robert told her unrepentantly.

"You repulse me," Ryder told him in return.

Advisor Robert clearly didn't care what Ryder thought of him, but he would care about this. Ryder punched Robert on the jaw, sending the sack of shit to the floor. "Not so tough without Afana, are you?"

Ryder and Massimo stepped into the lab, leaving Advisor Robert on the floor hugging his jaw.

Knuckles' neck creaked as he turned to them, his eyes were glowing red, and saliva drooling out of his mouth. He had the Madness. He growled at them and fought the restraints around his neck, wrists, and ankles.

"What have they done to him?" Ryder asked Massimo, but she didn't need an answer. There were blood samples around the lab, and Ivan's head was sitting in a puddle of melted ice. Afana had used Tank and Knuckles as test subjects, infecting them both with the Madness—and Knuckles, possibly, with Afana's own blood.

Massimo made a face at the mess that used to be Tank. "Looks like they have been trying to see if Afana is immune to the Madness. And by the look of that body, he's not."

Massimo shook his head at the state of the lab, which repulsed him. He turned away from it and stopped an old record player, which was broken. He moved the arm off the record to see what it was. "Opera!" he grumbled under his breath. He flipped through the vinyls that were next to it. "Show me Bee Gees… Come on, Bee Gees," he muttered as he went through them. "Dammit."

Fluffy came up next to Massimo and shook his head.

Massimo went over to Advisor Robert, who was still on the floor. "Does Afana have any more vinyl? I've been looking for a Bee Gees album for years."

"Afana likes the Bee Gees?" Robert repeated, looking like he had just eaten something bad.

"Yes, the Bee Gees—one of the greatest bands, along with ABBA and the Beatles. I could go on, but it's really not the time. So, does he have one?" Massimo pushed.

Advisor Robert flicked his wrist at the pile of slip-covers by the record player. "That's all he's got." He raised his finger and pointed to a room off the lab. "There may be some in there. That's Afana's living area."

Massimo walked toward the door, but Fluffy quickly got in front of it and growled at his dad. It could be a trap or just a distraction.

Massimo dropped his shoulders, knowing that he'd have to save that for later. He hoped he'd find at least one record he'd been dying to get his hands on in Afana's collection.

Ryder looked at the other severed heads. None of them belonged to Terrier or the women from Level Six, much to her relief.

"Is this a torture room?" Carter asked, his eyes widening as he entered the lab. The others were watching the advisors warily and keeping their weapons at the ready.

Ryder shrugged. "Something like that. I've checked the heads. Don't worry, hers isn't in here. And neither is Terrier's, which means that he'll be keeping Natalie and the others safe." Ryder knew he would have gone straight to Level Six once he got into the bunker to hide himself, but more importantly to protect the women and children. That was the Terrier Ryder had known since she was a child. He was driven to protect those who were weaker than him, just like Ryder.

It was time for her to be reunited with her best friend, and Carter with his sister.

Ryder clapped her hands. "Let's get the advisors locked in here, then get down to Level Six and free our friends!" Everyone followed her orders, even the advisors, although they were upset about being moved into a room with a Mad.

Ryder gave them a sharp look. "You can get in there with one restrained Mad, or you can go ahead of us and fight your way through the Mad below this level."

Advisor Robert wouldn't get up off the floor, so Carter dragged him in. Once the advisors were secured in the lab, Clint placed a chair in front of the door to stop them from getting out. All the advisors stood as far away from Knuckles as possible.

The plan had changed now for the better. Since all the cameras were out, they could make their way down to Level Six without Afana learning their location. Ryder considered their best move now, based on the new information. The plan had been for Massimo and Leandro to take on Afana, but since he wasn't there, they couldn't do it. Where *was* Afana? He wasn't a tiny animal hiding in a forest. He was a giant vampire with a thirst for killing. The blood smears on the floors made it impossible for Ryder and the others to see where he was, but soon they would find out.

"Keep your eyes out for Afana," said Ryder as they exited the lab.

"What does he look like?" Vicky asked. "Is he all good-looking like our Massimo?"

Ryder made a face as she tried to describe the mutant vampire to the others. "Fuck, no! Think of a giant cockroach, minus all the extra legs and things sticking out of his head. He has glowing red eyes like the Mad, and fangs like a vampire."

"Well, *he* sounds pretty, doesn't he?" said Graham, smiling at Carter.

"So, you've dumped me for a vampire insect now?" Carter responded somberly.

Graham snickered. "You dumped me for a vampire first. I thought you were happy with Massimo."

Ryder grinned at the two of them. "Another lovers' tiff? Graham's right. You dumped him for the upgraded Massimo."

Massimo looked at the two men. "I'm flattered, Carter. I really am. But you're just not my type."

Ryder had learned just what Massimo's type was from the magazine she had found when they were walking back to his home, and she couldn't wait to introduce him to Mama Lou in all her fineness. Those two would either be a match made in heaven, or they would fight like cats and dogs. The thought made Ryder laugh a little. Either way, it would be perfect when those two meet.

Carter shook his head and clutched his chest dramatically. "I've had my heart broken twice in one day. I don't know what I'm going to do now." He looked down through the glass floor and grinned wickedly. "I need something to do to distract myself. Any ideas?"

Clint had an idea. "How about looking down there at

the vampire we're going to kill?" He pointed down at Afana.

"He *does* look like a giant cockroach." Carter snickered. He could just make Afana out through the layers of blood-smeared glass.

Clint turned to Ryder. "I don't think he looks like a cockroach unless that's what cockroaches look like in this place." He grimaced at the thought and scanned the floor for cockroaches.

Vicky came over to stand with them. "I have to agree with Clint. He looks more like a giant rock man."

Ryder hadn't dared hope that Afana would be gone from the bunker when they'd made the plan to rescue Terrier and the others. She knew Afana was trapped in the bunker when it was light outside, and anyway, there was no way she would leave him alive to work his evil all over again.

Ryder had two emotions when it came to Afana: fear and anger. Anger was the stronger, and she was going to use that to win today. "I'd say he looks like a giant stinking shit, with steam drifting up from his head."

Carter joined in. "Nah." He squeezed his fingers together so it looked like Afana was between his fingers. "He looks like a tiny ant that's going to get squashed." Carter pushed his fingers together.

The other men started commenting on what he looked like as Ryder went to speak with Massimo. Leandro joined them. "It looks like Afana is down on Level Four. Now that the plan has changed, are you and Leandro still good taking on Afana while the rest of us go after the generals?"

Massimo nodded. "Yes. That plan works for me. And

remember to ask for us if you need us. Be careful, Ryder." Massimo patted her arm. "We have gotten used to your company, and I would hate to lose it so soon."

Ryder choked back the emotion Massimo's words caused. "You too, Massimo. You're a good friend and a good vampire."

Leandro pushed his head under Ryder's hand. His fur tickled her palm. He looked up at Ryder, his warm eyes connecting with hers. Her heart broke a little when she saw Leandro trapped inside Fluffy's body.

Ryder knelt and wrapped her arms around Leandro's neck. She whispered in his ear while she held him, "If we don't make it out of here, I… Thank you, Leandro. For being my friend and for helping me. Just be careful, and don't let Massimo get up to any mischief." She kissed Leandro on the snout. "Don't tell Carter. He shouldn't have to suffer three broken hearts in one day. You know he has a thing for big hunky men." Ryder smiled as she let go of Leandro.

With Ryder leading, the gang made their way down to Level Two, where the advisors and their families lived.

Carter stepped in front of Ryder as they got closer to the door. "I'll go first. We kinda need you to stay alive since you're our guide."

Carter was right, not that Ryder would admit it aloud. She moved to the side to let Carter go in front of her.

Carter grinned. "Let's do this." He turned to the door and glanced at Ryder. "I saw you trying to break my heart with Leandro. Not cool; not cool at all. You know I love that fluffball." He winked at Leandro.

Ryder turned to Fluffy and blew him kisses, then smiled at Carter. "Open the damn door, or I will."

"Have you been watching *The Italian Job*?" Massimo asked.

Ryder and Carter both looked at Massimo, confused.

"You know, Michael Caine?" Massimo asked.

"Michael Caine?" Ryder repeated blankly.

Carter frowned. "What's with the strange accent?"

Massimo rolled his eyes and waved his hand. "You'll know soon enough. Boy, I have loads of movies to share with you guys. Anyway, less dilly-dallying. Are we going to do this?"

"Oh, I'm ready all right." Carter opened the door to Level Two. As soon as the door was open a fraction, they heard the advisors' wives and children screaming.

Carter flung open the door the rest of the way, and the group quickly stepped onto Level Two, ready to attack. There were bodies on the floor with Mad hunched over them, eating with wet tearing sounds that turned the group's stomachs. The Madness was running wild on Level Two.

These Mad had been the advisors, and they had lived on this level with their families. Their lab coats were now splattered in blood. Some of the Mad had chunks bitten out of their cheeks, and others were gnawing on limbs they'd ripped from their victims. Ryder had no intention of her or any of her friends being a Mad's next meal.

Bloodcurdling screams came from a group of women and children, who were pinned up against a wall. They were trapped by the Mad coming at them from all angles.

Byrant instantly raised his guns, but Ryder shook her head in response, then placed her finger on her lip.

Ryder whispered to Byrant, "We have the upper hand. Afana doesn't know we're here, and we need to keep it that way."

Ryder smoothly drew an arrow from her quiver and nocked it as the others raised their weapons. The engraving on the arrowheads *was* really beautiful. Graham had done a fine job on them. Ryder knew she wouldn't miss. She never missed. Well, except once when she was drunk, but she was sober as a judge today thanks to Massimo's strong liquor.

She let out her breath and loosed the arrow, which flew silently through the air and landed in the back of a Mad's head. Ryder readied another arrow and fired, and Willard threw his knives. Within a few moments, the two of them had taken six Mad down.

When a dead Mad fell onto another, the other Mad took notice of what was happening and turned toward Ryder and her friends.

Arrows and knives flew across the bunker into the oncoming Mad, dropping them like flies. Blood oozed across the floor as Ryder and her friends made easy work of the Mad.

Ryder paused with her hands on her knees when they were done. She was out of breath, but the adrenaline pounded through her body.

Here's hoping that the rest of the bunker will be this easy.

Afana wanted to get to Level Six as quickly as possible to feed, since he hoped that the blood would counteract the infection carried by the two bites he'd received. He was afraid; more afraid than he'd ever been in his life. He thought about heading back to Level One, but having been a scientist in his former life, he would have spent hours running his blood and seeing if it was infected, and time would run out. He needed to be stronger. He needed more blood, and then the nanocytes in his body could fight off the infection.

Afana had sent the generals to Level Five to fight, and when he landed on Level Five through his personal drop hole with a thud, it took everyone on Level Five by surprise.

General Finn puffed his chest out and stepped closer. "Afana."

Afana looked around the level; they'd taken care of all

of the infected. *Finally, some people in here are doing their job,* Afana thought.

"Are they all dead?" Afana asked the general.

"Yes," Finn replied simply. He started to leave with the other generals.

"Stop!" Afana bellowed. A few of the men froze, but others continued to head toward the open door leading to the stairs to Level Four. *"STOP!"*

General Finn marched over to the men on the stairs. "Get back here now," he ordered through gritted teeth.

"No one leaves until I say so. Clean up the bodies!" Afana ordered. The men who were on the stairs headed back down toward the bodies. Afana wanted them to make sure everyone was dead to reduce his chance of getting bitten again.

When they piled the bodies up against the wall there was a rotten eggs smell coming from them, which was odd since some of them had only been killed a few minutes earlier. It didn't make sense that their bodies already smelled like week-old meat.

A few of the generals threw up from the smell and the sight. Some of the bodies were in tatters, ears and other parts ripped off, leaving bloody holes. There were bite marks that oozed blood, adding to the pool on the floor. They were well and truly fucked up, and it looked like they'd had tomato sauce poured over them.

The glass floor was now smeared with blood from the dragged bodies. There was also a pile of bodies over Afana's drop hole—the advisors Afana had thrown down. They decided to leave those there until told otherwise.

Those were Afana's bodies, and they didn't want to join them.

Normally bodies dropped through the hole would go all the way down to Level Six, but that wasn't the case today. The bodies had piled up on Level Five because the drop hole to Level Six was locked.

The surviving hunters who lived on Level Five were standing at the ends of their tunnels, watching from behind the barricades they'd hastily built.

"Walk with me," Afana said to General Finn, who looked like he was going to piss himself with excitement, then forced his face into a serious expression. General Finn walked like he had a stick up his ass as he followed Afana down the stairs past Level Five to the Level-Six door.

Afana pulled at the door handle to the Level Six exit, but it didn't open. The second time Afana used all his strength, and the sweat dripped down his face. It was like the door was welded to its frame.

The override Advisor Jones had implemented hadn't worked. Afana looked over Advisor Jones' body, his brains slopped on the glass floor beside the splintered mess. He'd smashed the head of the only man who could attempt to open the door. The other was locked *behind* the door.

Afana tried one more time to open the door and let out a scream that bounced off Level Five's walls when he failed. The men in the tunnels who had been watching quickly hid down their tunnels, out of Afana's sight. General Finn, on the other hand, stood there stock still. He didn't fear Afana, or if he did, he was doing a good job of hiding it.

"I want everyone from Level Six up on Level One, and I need you to get the men to do it," Afana told General Finn.

"Of course. I will do anything you request of me, and I will ensure that the men follow orders," General Finn said firmly. It actually looked like Afana was going to smile at Finn. Afana had gotten what he wanted.

Someone to do his dirty work.

"I will get the door opened," General Finn stated with conviction.

"How?" Afana asked between panting breaths.

General Finn indicated the spectators. "We can use the tools the men use to maintain the bunker. The tools are kept in one of the tunnels on this level."

Afana was getting annoyed that he was surrounded by idiots. "The door is unbreakable," Afana said dismissing General Finn as his hands clenched up.

"I wasn't thinking we should break the door. More like we take it apart," General Finn explained, and that got Afana's attention.

"Get to it," Afana ordered.

Afana looked up at Level Four. There were infected coming out of the tunnels he hadn't searched earlier. The generals were watching him, wondering what he was going to do next. This was *his* bunker, after all. He couldn't—and wouldn't—let the monsters have free rein with his cattle! He also didn't want to risk getting bitten again.

"Stay down here until you've opened the door or you'll be on top of the pile of bodies." With that, Afana ran for the stairs. He didn't have the energy to jump into the drop hole and pull his body up. He was worried that if he failed to make the leap, the generals would see that he was weaker than normal. All the fighting had sapped his energy.

Running up the stairs wore him down even more. He needed to head up to Level One just to feed. Afana began to wonder if it was blood he needed, or if he was just out of shape. This was the most fighting he'd ever done. He needed to get his house in order quickly.

Ryder walked over to the advisors' families. "You're free, so you can leave." She pointed to the door. The advisors' wives looked at one another, clearly not sure what to do. Many of them had had no choice who they'd been married to, although some had been lucky enough to find love in that brutal place. Most of the women had never been out of the bunker unless they were born outside. Now that they had the chance to escape, they didn't know what to do.

The women looked up through the glass ceiling at the advisors.

Some of the women took their kids' hands and led them past the bodies on the floor, shielding their eyes from the gore. Ryder and the others had two-tapped them; they weren't coming back to life after the Merry Men had taken care of them.

A woman came up to Ryder. "My husband?"

"We will let him out once we've rescued everyone,"

Ryder told her. She wasn't going to kill them, and neither were the Merry Men. They weren't as bad as Afana.

The rest of the women and kids left, and finally, Level Two was clear of Afana's hostages and the Mad.

When Ryder circled her finger in the air, the gang knew it was time to head to the next level.

Carter led them down the stairs to Level Three, and Ryder peered over his shoulder and saw that the door was open. Part of her was scared that the door would be closed behind her, but Carter winked at Ryder. "We're not going to be locked down here," he reassured her. "But if we are, what a cool group of people you get to hang out with!" Carter smiled, and so did the others.

Ryder winked back. "Good point. I couldn't think of a better group to hang out in a coffin with.".

Carter grinned. "I'll be able to teach you to braid your hair when it grows back."

Ryder ran a hand over her hair and laughed. "Hey, it'll be at my ears soon! Dustin, shut the door. I have to take Carter up on his offer."

Dustin frowned but headed back up the stairs.

"No," Ryder yelled.

Dustin froze.

"I was only joking," Ryder told him.

Carter shook his head. "Your comedic timing really sucks."

He's right. Ryder rolled her eyes. "I'm working on it."

Carter pushed open the door to Level Three, which was where the generals lived along with their wives and kids. There was no screaming on this level. Like Level Two there were bodies on the floor, only these were dressed in generals' uniforms. There were blockades at the entrances to their sleeping areas. Behind them were women and kids, who were looking at Ryder. She placed her finger on her lips.

One of the women yelped, "Derek!"

Gunshots came from behind them. The guards hiding in the staircase ambushed them. Bryant fired back at the guards, taking one down.

"No!" the woman yelled.

Should have kept her mouth shut, and the two of them could have been free. Ryder was pissed off.

There was no place for them to hide; they were out in the open. Shots were exchanged and when Kelvin was shot in the arm, he screamed in pain. The guards had too many guns, but her group had more weapons.

"Cover me!" Ryder yelled.

Ryder slammed her spear on the ground, and the sharp metal blades flew out. She ran at one of the guards and dropped, sliding across the bloody floor on her knees. She stabbed the general before he had a chance to fire at her, and pulled the spear out of him as he dropped down to his knees.

Then Ryder rolled her spear to the side, took her ankle knives, and threw them at two other guards. They landed in their necks.

More generals fell to the floor as the group killed them. There were only a few generals left, who ran back and hid behind the staircase.

"Don't shoot," one of them begged.

The woman from earlier shouted, "He said *don't* shoot!"

"Helena, hush," Another woman said to the loud-mouthed woman.

Ryder was getting really pissed off with the women on this level. They'd better shut up, or they'd end up like their husbands. "Will you be quiet?" Ryder yelled at Helena, then to the generals, "Drop your guns and slide them across to us."

Ryder could hear the generals speaking. It sounded like they were actually going to do it.

"Hand my gun to a *woman*? As *if.*" One of the generals pointed his gun at Ryder.

Ryder threw her spear at him as she ducked the bullet. The spear went through the general's head, and the bullet bounced off the glass wall. Ryder retrieved her spear after his body crashed to the floor.

The Merry Men took care of the other generals. A few of the women climbed over the barricades and ran to their husbands' bodies.

Helena had a wild look in her eyes. "You killed them. You killed *all* of them!" she yelled at them.

This one really doesn't listen, thought Ryder.

"You're free now, and you can leave the bunker," Ryder told all the women. They didn't move. "I said, you're free."

Still nothing.

Helena looked at Ryder with disgust. "We don't *want* to leave. This is our home."

Helena had clearly been brainwashed by their captors. The generals' wives had a very different life to the women on Level Six; an almost normal life. Ryder knew she wouldn't get the same response on Level Six, where the women were no more than commodities to be handed out as favors to those who pleased Afana.

Ryder shrugged and turned to the others. "Whatever. Come on, let's get those out who want to be free."

Helena got in Ryder's face, waving a finger. "How dare you come in here and kill our men and ruin our home! How *dare* you! *Afana!*" she screamed.

Vicky pursed her lips at the outburst. "Will someone shut that nagging bitch up before the fucking vampire hears her?"

Everyone looked down through the glass floor at Level Four where they'd last seen Afana, but they could no longer see his giant figure. He could be down any one of the tunnels or on one of the other levels.

Ryder quickly turned to the other women and kids behind the barricade. They weren't moving or saying a thing. Helena was the only mouthy one, and they needed to shut her up.

She needed a bandage. Ryder unwrapped the one she'd used after donating blood to Massimo, then the other one from the fight with Sergei.

"Turn her around," Ryder told Carter. He did as she requested, and Ryder tied the bandage around Helena's wrists. Then she turned her around. "This will shut you up," Ryder said as she gagged the woman, whose eyes were wild. "When we're gone, go over to the others and get them to untie you. I don't want you to be defenseless with the Mad around."

Helena rolled her eyes.

Bitch.

Ryder and the others retrieved their weapons. "I'm over this ungrateful level. Let's bounce."

Carter whooped. "Fucking *yeah.*"

When they all got to the stairs, the lights flickered. Everyone looked at one another.

Ryder stopped in her tracks. "What the fuck is going on? The lights never go on and off." She waited to see if it happened again, but it didn't. She shrugged. "I guess today isn't a normal day since the bunker is under attack from all sides." Ryder looked up at Level One. The advisors were out of the lab, and their wives were there with them. Ryder had thought they would have just run outside, but they'd gone straight to their husbands and freed them. Ryder had underestimated the women's bonds with their husbands.

Advisor Robert was looking down at Ryder with a devilish grin on his face, but the cameras and audio were off so he couldn't warn Afana.

But he could do one thing to help him.

He wiggled his fingers at Ryder and flicked a switch which plunged them into darkness.

***

Level Six was inky-black.

The children screamed in fear of the dark.

The kids weren't the only ones who were afraid. "What's going on?" Terrier demanded. "What happened to the lights?"

Mama Lou's voice trembled in the dark. "I don't know. This has never happened. The question is, how we are going to separate the bitten if we can't see anyone?"

"We have to try," Terrier answered.

"Those who have been bitten, we need to get you into the rooms so you can rest," Mama Lou said, as if she were thinking the same thing as Terrier. "Can you make your way over carefully so we can get you into a bed and looked after?"

Terrier and the others headed in the direction of the bitten, and collectively they froze, but a pair of glowing red eyes beamed like headlights in the darkness behind them.

"One of them has turned," Terrier shouted, and his cries out were followed by others. Luckily the kids and Natalie were safely in the kids' room. Terrier could use force to stop the infected without scaring them.

"General Murray, shoot it," Mama Lou ordered.

Before Murray could shoot, the eyes disappeared. *Were they getting smarter?* Terrier feared for their chances if that was true. Screams came from the direction of where they'd seen the glowing eyes. The infected had just bitten its first victim.

Chaos erupted in the darkness as people tried to flee the danger.

The red eyes flashed again.

"Now!" Mama Lou shouted.

Murray pointed the gun in the direction of the eyes and fired. The glowing red eyes disappeared again, this time because the infected was dead. They knew this because of the thud of the dead body on the floor.

"All bitten, into the rooms *now*! If you don't move, you will be shot!" Mama Lou spoke sternly. The injured hugged the wall to guide them to the rooms. They weren't going to risk that Mama Lou was bluffing.

It took a few moments for everyone's eyes to adjust to the darkness. "Well, that was unexpected," Ryder said.

"Graham, have you got any night-vision glasses?" Massimo asked

The silence between the men made it clear that no one else had a clue what Massimo was talking about. "Night *what*?"

"It was a shot in the dark," Massimo admitted, laughing. Then he began to sing quietly. "*Night fever, night feverrrrr...*"

Ryder grinned. He had a song for everything, and he was one talented singer.

"*And I'm glowing in the dark, Willy Wonka...* That's not right." Massimo huffed. "I really need to get the vinyl." He kept singing under his breath, then stopping himself. Massimo couldn't get the words right.

There must be a way to get him the vinyl. It's the least I can do. Ryder made a note to herself. "Once we take care of

Afana and free everyone, we'll find you the Bee Gees record," she told Massimo.

"You really are a sweetheart," Massimo told her.

"Look down there," Koda interrupted.

Everyone looked down at Level Four, although it was darker than night. Level Four was where the hunters lived. There were two glowing red eyes, then two more, and even more. The level was riddled with the Mad.

They were just slowly moving around, not going after anyone. "Those wrinkled ass-lickers. We can't see Afana anymore." Ryder was more than a bit annoyed.

Massimo laid a hand on her shoulder. "But he can't see us, either. We'll lead. Stick to the plan."

Massimo was right; they could use the darkness in their favor. "Okay," she conceded.

Massimo pushed open the door, and Leandro followed him down the stairs. The others followed them, and Ryder's heart pounded as their boots thudded on the steps. They were going deeper into the heart of Hell, and soon they would be facing the devil himself. She gripped her knives. She would be ready for anything that came at her.

The only good thing with the darkness was that she could aim for the glowing red eyes of the Mad as if they were a bulls-eye.

Massimo and Leandro peeled off and disappeared into the darkness as they passed Level Four. They looked back just once, then left the stairs as the others made their way down to Level Five.

The glowing red eyes were moving slowly. They weren't in any hurry to get anywhere. They hadn't noticed the intrusion. It was like they were just hanging around waiting for their next kill, which sure wasn't going to be any of them. They were a badass killing group. A few Mad were no challenge for them.

It was the real monster they needed to fear and find. They needed to fear him so they could defeat him.

The smart and strong would win, and the overgrown jerkoffs were going to die!

Massimo's heart was racing quickly as he and Leandro entered the main section of Level Four where they'd spotted Afana. Ryder had said Afana looked like a giant cockroach, but Massimo thought he looked more like the Incredible Hulk, just not green. There was a red filter over the other vampire because of the glass-spattered layers they had to look through to see him. Massimo hoped that the in-person version of Afana would be small like an insect. With that thought and the Bee Gees singing in his mind to give him courage, he moved gingerly forward.

Leandro was by his side. He was glad his son was with him and that they would fight the beast together, father and son. He was also a little scared, since it was his job to keep his son safe. Massimo knew that if he'd refused to let Leandro help he would have come anyway, so he didn't argue. Massimo brushed his hand over Leandro's back, and the wolf looked up at his Pops.

They were both ready for the fight.

They came upon their first Mad. He looked into the darkness, swaying a little as he awkwardly lurched forward, then he turned randomly and shuffled off in a different direction. The Mad didn't know where he was going, or why.

Massimo noticed that the other Mad were the same. The pair moved silently through the level to find Afana. *How on earth could such a monster be hiding in the shadows? Maybe he really* was *the size of an ant?* Massimo spotted the lights ahead.

The *red* lights.

Oh no, he wasn't.

Bright red beams appeared out of one of the tunnels, and they were much higher than the Mad's. This was Afana, and he was massive.

Massimo realized his eyes would be glowing red as well since he was in his vampire form. This was a good thing, because he could pass himself off as a Mad. Leandro's eyes were orange, and he was much shorter than the other Mad. Massimo stood in front of Leandro to hide his eyes.

Afana turned and looked straight at Massimo.

Here goes nothing, Massimo thought. "Hey, Afana! I was told you lived here now, and I thought I'd pop in for a cup of sugar. Oh, and do you have a Bee Gees album I could borrow? It has been years since I could listen to them, and I keep forgetting the words."

Massimo felt Leandro's tail brush the back of his legs as he moved around him, he was using the Mad for cover, which didn't last long. Massimo's voice woke them up, and they were going for Massimo and Afana.

Afana and Massimo made short work of killing the Mad. Bodies were thrown all around the level until there were none left standing.

Massimo caught a glimmer of Leandro's eyes. He was at

the end of one of the tunnels behind Afana, in place to attack.

An awkward silence fell between the vampires in the aftermath of the killing.

"What? Who's that?" Afana asked in a dark, gravelly voice.

"It's Massimo. Remember me? Your vampire buddy before the WWDE?" Massimo kept his voice light.

"Massimo?" Afana sounded confused.

Massimo laughed. "Yep. The one and only. I didn't know you were alive. I thought Bethany Anne killed you when she was going around killing the Forsaken. I guess you were the Forgotten, like me."

Afana strode forward. "Forgotten?" He huffed. "I'm not forgotten. Her kind is the reason I'm trapped in here!" Afana spat. His breath smelled like a washed-up rotting whale. Massimo did everything he could to keep from gagging.

"Well, I see you made the most of it with your cool bunker. *Do* you have any Bee Gees records?" Massimo asked. *If he tells me, it will save me loads of time looking for them when he's dead.*

Afana was pissed off. "Why the hell of all records would I have the Bee Gees? I have class, unlike you. You always did have terrible taste in music."

"Oh, Afana. In all our years I've heard you say some incorrect things, but that one has to go on top of the list," Massimo replied.

Afana began to breathe in and out heavily. He was getting annoyed. Afana's breath was still repulsive, but it was clear that Massimo's plan to unbalance the other vampire was working. "List? Bee Gees? What the hell are you doing here?"

Stalling time is over. I hope Ryder and the others have gotten to Level Six. Massimo dropped the act. "I'm here to clean out the Madness." Massimo rushed at Afana. "And I'm here to take care of you!" He slammed into the other vampire. At the same time, Leandro leaped into the back of Afana's legs, and the mutant vampire toppled.

Massimo took full advantage. He dived on top of Afana and began punching. Massimo was stronger than Afana, which took both vampires by surprise. Leandro dug his jaws into Afana's legs, clamping down on them to stop him from struggling. He wasn't going to let go, not while his Pops was winning the fight against the overgrown monster.

Afana flopped like a fish beneath Massimo and finally managed to free his arm. He began hitting back, but Massimo didn't budge. It didn't matter how many punches he threw, Massimo would be the victor here today.

Afana lashed out with his foot, kicking Fluffy across the room. Fluffy landed awkwardly and let out a whine to tell Massimo he was okay.

Massimo was enraged. "You will *not* hit my son!"

Massimo stood and dragged Afana to his feet, then hit him with a punch that came all the way from his toes. Afana dropped like a sack of potatoes.

Massimo leaned down to his son. "Leandro, are you okay?" Massimo's voice was full of concern.

Leandro let out a howl. Luckily Weres healed fast.

Massimo waved his fists in the air and did a Mohammad Ali-style dance around Afana's prone body.

"And the crowd went *wiiild!*" As he cheered for himself, he felt a hundred years younger. No, that wasn't true. It was more like *two* hundred.

"I *said,* the crowd went *wild,*" he repeated to the oncoming Mad, whom neither he nor Afana had two-tapped. *Time to bust out the badass vampire again!* Massimo got busy and two-tapped all of the Mad until there were no more red glowing eyes and he was sure that they weren't coming back after the ass-kicking he had just given them.

Massimo let out a sigh; all this ass-kicking had drained his energy. No wonder Afana was weak, after all of the people he'd fought with.

Leandro growled. "What is it?" Massimo the scanned the room.

Massimo could just make out movement above them. That overgrown elephant turd was climbing to the next level through a hole in the ceiling. Before Massimo and Leandro could get to him, he shut the glass door and resumed climbing up the shaft. They would have to use the stairs to get to Afana.

"Ryder was right, he's a cockroach! One I'm going to step on!" Massimo stormed over to the staircase and up to Level Three, which was still pitch-black, making it damn near impossible to spot him. Massimo had a feeling he knew where Afana was going. He needed to feed, and if he reached Level One and fed on one of the people there, he would be stronger than Massimo.

Massimo had to stop him.

Ryder and the others descended the stairs to Level Five. This was another floor on which the men lived, the one Ryder had lived on with Terrier.

Carter pushed open the door a little and stepped back, gagging. "What the fuck is that?" he choked. "It smells like a box of smashed assholes in there!" He covered his nose and mouth with a sleeve and led them into the level.

It was a place which none of them wanted to be near. *We need some fucking lights,* Ryder thought. The inky darkness of the bunker and the smell of death all around them was making the bunker even eerier, something Ryder hadn't thought possible. *We just need to get through this level, and then we're at Level Six.*

Ryder heard a click of a gun and raised her hand, hoping the others would be able to see it. She grabbed Carter, pulling him back, and the door slowly closed behind them. "There are generals on this floor," Ryder whispered.

Carter's voice was muffled through his sleeve. "I thought the generals lived on Level…Three. Didn't we just take care of them all?"

"They do, but Afana may have sent some of them down if there was a Mad breakout, so there could be Mad *and* generals." Ryder shrugged. "Fuck, there could be Mad generals, for all I know."

Clint stepped forward. "Sounds like the kind of fight I like."

Ryder drew an arrow from her quiver and nocked it, then motioned toward the level with her bow. "Be my guest."

They were momentarily blinded when the lights flickered back to life. The advisors on Level One had turned them back on. Everyone shielded their eyes, their night vision destroyed by the harsh glare.

Ryder blinked the pain away, and when she opened her eyes, she was met by the barrels of the generals' weapons. *Shit.*

Her bow was already raised, so she shifted to aim at the general in front of her, and the others did the same. The standoff was tense. The numbers were even, and the weapons were pretty well matched. Ryder knew all the generals. The one in front of her was one of the slimier jerks, General Finn. Ryder looked around for General Murray, the highest-ranking general. He wasn't there. Maybe he'd finally gotten what was coming to him.

Ryder peered through the glass floor when movement caught her eye. It was Terrier, and he was grinning up at her. Beside him was General Murray. *That greasy flea on a rat's back! What the hell is he doing down there? And why hasn't Terrier killed him?*

They were standing together like friends, for fuck's sake! General Murray had put most of them in the bunker, and now the bastard was standing with them? Ryder shook it off. She couldn't let herself be distracted, not when she was so close to her goal. She had to focus on the task at hand, which was getting rid of the assholes in front of her.

That split-second lapse had cost Ryder the advantage, and the generals opened fire on the Merry Men. Ryder and the others dived out of the way. She hit the floor and rolled to her feet, then scanned the others. No one had been hit, thankfully. She'd have to deal with General Murray later.

The Merry Men didn't have much to use as cover other than the tables and chairs in the middle of the Level Five common area, but then they weren't planning on staying there very long.

Ryder bobbed up and loosed an arrow, and the fight was on. The generals had no combat skills to speak of. They'd been trained to rely on their guns to keep order. Ryder knew this and made a game of aiming for the generals' gun hands. The light caught Willard's knife as it flew through the air and landed in the throat of one of the generals. "Nice shot!" Ryder called. "A few more of them and we'll be golden."

Ryder retrieved her arrows as she worked her way around the common area. Each one she pulled from a dead general she sent off again to make another dead general. She was finally getting her revenge on the fuckers who'd kidnapped her when she was a kid. *They aren't going to do it to anyone else,* Ryder thought.

"Kill them. Kill *all* of them!" Ryder yelled, not that the Merry Men needed the order. They were doing a fine job without her instruction.

General Finn had escaped Ryder's arrows so far. "Get that fucking bitch!" he screamed, red-faced. His bleeding hand was shaking with so much rage he was unable to keep his gun straight. He fired and missed, shooting one of the other generals by mistake.

Ryder grinned. "Nice, Finn. If I'd known you would do the job for me, I wouldn't have bothered coming back to this shithole."

General Finn's face turned purple. "You shouldn't even be up here! Get back down to Level Six with the other whores!" He pulled the trigger four times in quick succession. "Or you can die!"

Shit! Ryder dropped and rolled out of the way of the oncoming bullets. Three flew over her head, but one left a hot line and a trickle of blood on her arm. She'd had worse. Her adrenaline was high, and she wasn't going to let a little scrape stop her.

The Merry Men weren't going to take that.

Vicky swung her shovel and General Finn collapsed unconscious to the floor, bleeding profusely from the gash across his face. They turned their attention back to mopping up the nearby generals. Vicky used her shovel to block the bullets fired at her, then swung it to impact with the closest general's head. There was a crunch when it connected with his skull, and the force lifted him off his feet and onto the floor, never to get up again.

Graham yelled, "Watch your back, Vicky!"

Another general had turned to shoot her. Graham sent

his axe spinning through the air to land in the general's shoulder. It embedded itself deep into the muscle, and only stopped when it got wedged in his bone. The thought of the pain made Ryder wince, but he'd deserved it.

They *all* deserved it.

The general stumbled sideways and reached up to pull out the axe, but before he could get his hand on it Vicky's shovel met his face with a sickening crunch.

Vicky kicked the general on his way down and smiled gratefully at Graham.

The Merry Men drove the rapidly-dwindling group of generals back. Ryder and the others with knives were making quick work of killing them. Ryder knew that soon the generals would be out of bullets. They just needed to last that long.

Carter danced in a circle with a tall, thin general and they traded blows, Carter getting his licks in. Another general moved to flank Carter, but she stopped that shit right in its tracks with a well-placed arrow to the eye. Ryder elbowed a passing general in the face as she crossed to assist her friend.

Carter didn't need her help, landing a sweet right hook that broke the general's jaw. Ryder didn't want to be left out. She ran over and winked at Carter as she swung a foot up into the general's crotch, then moved past the two of them to take out the generals she'd chosen as her next targets. Carter's general didn't know what had hit him, but he did once Ryder's boot connected with his junk. He dropped to his knees, whimpering in pain.

Carter came over and gave Ryder a fist-bump. "Nice moves."

She accepted the gesture with a grin. "Thank you. I was going to say the same to you."

Graham sighed dramatically. "You two are breaking my heart. Why can't you just settle down, Carter?" He wiggled his eyebrows suggestively. "Maybe the three of us could settle down *together* sometime…"

Ryder snickered and rolled her eyes. "Honestly, of all the times and places to reignite the bromance."

The fight was pretty much over. The few remaining generals held up their hands and surrendered, not so tough when they ran out of bullets. The Merry Men got to work tying the generals up.

"Sorry, you two aren't my type," Ryder told Graham and Carter as she bound the general's hands behind his back with his own shirt.

Both men clutched their hearts and Carter went the extra mile for dramatic effect as usual. "Say it isn't so, Ryder. What can I do to earn your love?"

The generals looked at Ryder and her friends as they continued their banter.

Vicky snickered. "Ryder goes for the *fluffy* type."

Ryder rolled her eyes. "Keep your eyes on them. I'll get the door and free everyone on Level Six. Nice work, guys." Ryder smiled as she walked down the stairs to the door and pulled on it, but the door it wouldn't open.

"Carter, give us a hand." Ryder's request was greeted by a round of applause from Carter as he headed toward her.

It was firmly locked.

Ryder tried it again, then went back up to Level Five. "*Shit*. Massimo might know how to open the door. He knows all the technology stuff." Carter nodded, and Ryder looked at the glass ceiling. There was activity on Level Four—a few generals who must have been down the tunnels when they passed through the level. And there were Mad.

Ryder turned to her team. "Willard and Koda, can you find Massimo and tell him that we can't get into Level Six? We need him to get the door open. Be careful, there are Mad and generals on that level."

"Got you," Willard replied. Koda just nodded. The two men ran for the stairs to find Massimo.

General Finn had regained consciousness. He struggled to his feet and glared at Willard and Koda, missing the gravity of the generals' situation completely. "Stop them!" he screamed.

The other generals looked at Ryder and her friends, not sure what to do. They were weaponless and now outnumbered.

Ryder's lip curled, and she shook her head at Finn in disgust. "It's over. Stop ordering them to do Afana's dirty work."

"It's not his dirty work. It's to keep our civilization alive. It's great work, not dirty work!" General Finn spoke with such passion Ryder knew that he truly believed every word of what he'd just said.

Clint laid a stunning haymaker across the general's jaw. General Finn was unconscious before he hit the ground.

"Damn…" Rang out from both groups.

Clint rolled his shoulders. "Time for you young ones to learn a lesson from an old-timer. *That's* how you knock out an ass-licking skeleton like that motherfucker."

"I think I've got a semi-on." Carter grinned smugly.

Ryder smirked. "You get semi-ons at the oddest times. Do you need Graham to give you a hand, or you good to get on with the job?"

Carter looked down at his bulge, then winked at Ryder. "What do *you* think? Door first."

Terrier spotted Ryder looking at him through the glass ceiling.

She's fucking done it! Terrier thought. She'd come back to the bunker to rescue everyone.

He felt relief wash over him, but they weren't out of the woods yet. Terrier had a lot of hope that Ryder and the people she'd brought with her would get them out of there, since they'd already made it through five levels. He had worried that if Ryder *did* return, the generals would kill her before she ever reached him.

Instead, she'd fought off the Mad and the generals. He'd always known that Ryder could face anything that was thrown at her and come out on top.

Terrier pumped his fist in the air. "We're waiting for you, Ryder!" he shouted. "You've got this!"

Ryder glanced at the level above where they'd left Massimo and Fluffy, along with a pack of Mad and Afana. Ryder hoped they were okay. It was really hard to see anything with all the blood smeared across the glass. *They had to be all right.*

She looked back down at Terrier, who had a huge grin on his face. He pumped the air with a fist and shouted something she couldn't hear. Ryder grinned back mirroring his gesture. "I'm coming for you all, Terrier! Hang on just a bit longer!"

Time to set her friends free.

Koda led the way back up the stairs to find Massimo, with Willard close behind him. The two men climbed the stairs two at a time, trying frantically to stay out of the Mad's reach. The men made it back to Level Four, where they'd left Massimo and Fluffy to kill Afana.

Koda nodded at Willard. Willard had his knives up and ready to throw as Koda opened the door.

Koda opened it a fraction and peeked into the level, but the door was flung open before Koda could release his grip. He was pulled into Level Four and the arms of the waiting Mad. The Mad were no longer waiting for fresh flesh to sink their teeth into, their meal had arrived.

The Mad flung the door open and headed straight for Willard. Willard threw some of his knives but missed in his panic. Willard had nowhere to go except back down the stairs Level Five, where Ryder and the others were.

Fear flooded Willard's body. He didn't want to turn into

a Mad like Javier. The Mad was fast, and its arms were stretched out as it tried to grab Willard.

Willard glanced over his shoulder as he ducked out of the way, and his feet betrayed him. They tangled on one another, and he went ass over teakettle down the stairs.

"Mad! Mad!" Willard yelled it over and over as he crashed down the stairs and slammed into the closed door to Level Five.

The Mad didn't stop. It almost flew down the stairs as the need to bite into Willard took over.

Willard screamed and tried to get hold of the door handle, but he couldn't get a grip on it.

The Mad landed on Willard, knocking the breath out him. *This is where I'm going to die.*

The door to Level Five was flung open, dropping Willard and the Mad down the last few stairs and into Level Five. The Mad lunged in an attempt to bite Willard's neck, but before it could a size-eight black boot connected with the Mad's jaw and knocked it off Willard with force.

Willard scrambled across the floor away from the Mad. His body was bruised and battered, but there was no way he was going to stay anywhere near the Mad. He had more knives ready for any other Mad.

The generals on the level ran away from the Mad, since they were weaponless and scared.

"Hey, *dickhead,*" Ryder yelled at the Mad. It and all the generals turned to look at Ryder. Ryder grinned. "Just the Mad dickhead for now," she told the generals. "I'll deal with *you* dickheads later.".

Ryder ran at the Mad, her spear blade activated and ready to strike it. She plunged the spear into the Mad's overgrown gut and regretted it instantly. The Mad gripped the spear and swung around, and Ryder had to let go of it. The Mad came back at Ryder with her spear sticking out of its bloody guts.

"Hey, I *like* that spear!" Ryder wanted it back.

Carter was at Ryder's side before she even had to ask, his axes up and ready to chop off the fat Mad's head. "Are you going to let me kill this one?" Carter asked.

Ryder shrugged and stepped to the side. "Be my guest."

Carter happily accepted and ran at the Mad. His first axe missed the Mad's neck and sliced across its face. Carter's next axe was ready, and this time he didn't miss. He went for the throat, and blood sprayed out of the open wound, covering Carter.

Carter tried to get away from the blood splatters, but the Mad wasn't finished just yet. He still wanted to feed. Every time Carter moved, the Mad came after him.

"Go the other way," Ryder yelled, trying to help him get away from the blood fountain.

Carter dodged again. "I'm *trying*. Will one of you two-tap him!"

Ryder folded her arms and grinned. "I thought it was *your* kill. Come on, I want my spear back."

Carter was now running in circles. "As soon as it runs out of blood I'll get it for you!" Carter bitched. "Surely this Mad will be out of blood soon?"

Then again, it was one fat Mad, Ryder thought.

"It's yours now," Carter said as he headed toward the gang. None of them wanted to be covered in the fat Mad's blood, even though they already all had a fair amount of blood on them. They all looked like they'd taken a shower in blood instead of water.

Byrant fired his gun at an oncoming Mad, and it dropped to the ground. A fountain of the Mad's blood sprayed upwards toward Level Four.

Ryder spun. "Where's Koda?"

"On Level Four," Willard replied breathlessly. "Help him."

No one wasted any time. They sprinted up the stairs to Level Four to help Koda. Ryder sprinted toward the Mad and went to pull the spear from his dead body.

"Not so fast." General Finn's nasal voice came from behind them.

Ryder whirled to see the general's gun pointing straight at her head.

***

Even through the blood-smeared ceiling, Terrier could see the situation unfolding above him. Ryder was on her own with the generals. He'd screamed up at her, trying to warn her that she was in danger. He'd waved his arms frantically, and everyone else on Level Six was doing the same, but she didn't see.

They'd all been so happy to see Ryder and the group of strangers. They'd had real hope for the first time that they were going to get off Level Six and out of the bunker to freedom. For Terrier, it was worse than that. Ryder had come back for Terrier as she'd promised, only to be captured again.

"We've got to open the door! We need to help Ryder."

Terrier pleaded with everyone. They all looked at him skeptically. No one knew how to open the door other than Advisor George, and he was locked up. He glared at the door to the room where Advisor George was being kept. "I've got to get the answer out of him." Terrier dashed over to the door.

Peter blocked Terrier's way. "I'm sorry, man. I can't let you do that." Peter held up his hands to show he wasn't happy with the situation. The two giants stood eyeballing one another.

"I *have* to. They'll kill Ryder if we can't get the door open." The thought of anyone harming Ryder terrified Terrier, since he'd sworn to protect her. He wasn't going to stand by and watch it happen, not to his Ryder. "Step aside, Peter," Terrier ordered.

"Terrier, you know you won't be able to get any sense out of Advisor George. He's Mad. The Mad don't talk, they only groan for flesh. And if you open the door, he will escape and kill others. Do you think Ryder would want you to free a Mad for the sake of her life? I know she wouldn't. You can't risk the whole level for Ryder."

Terrier knew Peter was right, but it didn't make it any easier to hear. He didn't know what to do. When he looked at the glass ceiling again, the generals were all in front of her, and there was no one to protect her.

"There has to be a way." Murray came to stand alongside Terrier.

The former general's forehead crinkled in thought. "Terrier's right, they will kill her. Especially that prick Finn. I only stayed in charge so he couldn't take over. The guy's a monster." He ignored Peter's glare. "Maybe

Samantha knows how to open the door. She was able to do it once when she tried to escape, and you rescued her."

He was right—Samantha *had* done it once before. Terrier wasn't sure. "That was before Advisor George messed around with the wires to override Afana's system." Terrier hung his head in disappointment.

General Murray shrugged. "She knew the numbers from watching, so maybe she was watching when Advisor George did the override. Worth a try, isn't it?"

"Yes, it is," Mama Lou agreed. She joined the men in watching the ceiling. "Anything we can do to save Ryder's life is worth a try." She headed straight to the kids' room and the men quickly followed.

Ryder didn't have much chance on her own. She was a damn good fighter, one of the best Terrier had seen. However, Finn was a vicious bastard, one who served Afana's evil will happily.

Mama Lou knocked on the door to the kids' room, both because she didn't want to startle them by marching in after the last few days, and also the door was locked as she'd requested. "It's Mama Lou and my friends," Mama Lou called.

Jasmine opened the door with her bed pole firmly gripped in her hand as though she thought a Mad would knock. She scanned behind Mama Lou and opened the door.

"Samantha, may I have a word with you?" Mama Lou asked gently, trying not to scare her. Samantha had been through a lot more than the rest of the kids. The child had witnessed some horrific sights on the higher levels when the outbreaks had happened.

Samantha gingerly walked over to Mama Lou with her head down. "You're not in trouble. We need your help," Mama Lou told her.

Samantha raised her tiny head, and her big brown eyes looked into Mama Lou's. "M-my help?"

Mama Lou nodded and smiled at the little girl. "Yes, your help. Were you watching Advisor George when he was playing around with the wires?" Samantha nervously twisted her long brown hair between her fingers and Mama Lou patted her shoulder gently. "Really, you're not in trouble. Ryder's here and she wants to see us, but we can't open the door."

Samantha looked at Mama Lou oddly. "Mama Lou, you used the wrong word, silly. Ryder is a boy. You should be saying he, not *she*." Samantha laughed, which warmed Mama Lou's heart. She knew that Samantha would get through today and live a better life. Once they got her out of here, she'd be able to put it all behind her and not dwell on the past.

"Ryder was pretending to be a he so she could go outside," Mama Lou explained, much to the joy of the children listening.

"I was thinking of doing that," Rebecca announced proudly, "and *he* said it wouldn't work!" She pointed at Luke, whose mouth fell open.

Mama Lou sniffed with emotion. "No one will have to pretend to be something they're not once we get out of this level. Samantha, it's really important. Do you know how to fix the wires?"

Samantha looked up at Murray with frightened eyes.

He knelt to be at Samantha's eye-level. "I promise you

won't be in trouble, and that I will help you and your friends be free. I'm the one who should be in trouble for not helping you earlier. I'm sorry."

Samantha stared at Murray like she was memorizing every wrinkle on his face. "Mama Lou says that if someone says they are sorry and they mean it, then you should accept it. I believe you." She nodded. "And that if you make a promise, you can't break it. Pinky promise," she added, holding her finger out to Murray.

He remembered doing the pinky promise with Martin when he was little. The kids learned it down on Level Six, and they never forgot it.

General Murray's stuck his little finger out, and Samantha wrapped her finger around his and smiled. "I know what Advisor George did to the wires, and I think I can show you how to fix them."

The generals who had been tied up regained their confidence when General Finn took charge again. They gathered in front of Ryder, who turned to make a snarky comment to Carter and realized that everyone had gone to Level Four, leaving her alone with the generals. They looked pissed, and so was Ryder. Did they really think they could get one over on her just because she was alone and outnumbered?

Ryder went for her spear. "Shut the fuck up, Finn." She'd wanted to say that to him for years. That sharp, pointy nose was stuck so far up Afana's asshole that when the vampire opened his mouth, you'd be able to see the tip of it. He had just been waiting for a chance like this when General Murray wasn't here, so he could step up and be the biggest jerk.

"Get her," General Finn told the remaining generals. Now that the odds were a little more favorable, they actually listened.

Ryder boiled with anger. "Don't you touch me." She pointed at the generals surrounding her.

They looked at her warily, then at General Finn, whose eyes were bulging. "What are you waiting for?" The men tried to grab Ryder, but she was quicker than the generals. She punched the nearest one in the nose, wishing he was General Finn since she wanted to break *his* sharp nose. His time would come!

Ryder swung for the next general, who ducked out of the way. His didn't miss and it connected with Ryder's ribs, which were still burning from the fight with Sergei. She wasn't going to let the generals know she was in pain. Her years in the bunker had taught her to hide any weakness that would get her killed.

Ryder returned his punch with another, this one was a better shot that landed in his ribs. The general was strong, and he wasn't in pain like Ryder. He doubled and recovered, but Ryder had thrown that one as a distraction to get him looking down for a moment. Ryder scored another punch right in General Dickhead's face, and Ryder knew that one stung him like a motherfucker. His jaw snapped sideways, but Ryder wasn't done. She launched herself at him and followed up with more punches.

Hands gripped Ryder's arms, stopping her from punching General Dickhead anymore. She fought against the generals who were dragging her back and kicked at General Dickhead. He was able to move out of the way, since unlike Ryder he wasn't being held back by a group of overzealous men.

She thrashed, and their grips tightened. She sneered at Finn. "Hey, General Fuckface, getting others to do your work for you again? Why don't you fight me on your own? Or are you scared?" One of the generals pulled her bow and quiver off her back and threw them across the floor. Those idiots! "You better hope you didn't break my bow, asshole."

General Finn moved closer to Ryder and narrowed his eyes, which were already mostly shut from the swelling in his ruined face. Ryder laughed at him. "How can you even see me?"

"I can see you well enough." He grunted. "Let her go. She's mine." General Finn waved them off, and the other generals did as they were told.

Something—no some*one*—caught Ryder's eyes. The men on Level Five, the ones she'd lived and worked with, looked surprised. They'd never seen Ryder as a female, and they'd never seen anyone stand up to the generals like she was doing. She wasn't sure if they were going to be on the generals' side or hers. Possibly neither, since they were just standing by and watching. One person wasn't paying attention, Decso. He was pointing at the floor.

Ryder glanced to where Decso was looking, it was a pile of Mad bodies. Finn punched Ryder in the gut, sending her backward, and she gasped. A few men from her level cheered. Dammit, she'd known them all of her life, those *jerks!* Was Decso just trying to distract her to give General Finn an easy target? She'd finish Decso off after General Finn was dead.

She wasn't going to let Finn throw all the good punches. "Is that all you've got?" She spat blood at him. "Fucking pathetic."

"Hold her. Once we've gotten rid of you, we'll move on to

your friends." He grinned, looking down at the floor and then up at the ceiling. She had friends trapped on both levels now.

The generals came back to grab Ryder and she tried to get away, but she couldn't. They had her.

"Hey, that's not fair!" Decso yelled. "Look, they are cheating. They are holding Ryder's arms stopping her from fighting." A few were nodding with Decso, some were scratching their heads, and others were questioning how they hadn't worked out that Ryder wasn't a man.

While Decso was distracting General Finn and the other generals, Ryder looked to where Decso was pointing. He was trying to help her. By one of the Mad bodies there was a knife, which was hard to see because it was covered in blood and guts.

She needed to get to the knife.

General Finn hit her in the jaw, and she sagged in the arms of the generals restraining her as a black wave washed over her vision.

"The knife, Decso. Get me the knife," Ryder pleaded between punches. Decso stared at her, scared. A part of him wanted to get it, but the other part didn't know what to do. "Decso, *please!*"

Decso got a look of determination in his eyes. He was going to help, so she could take a few more punches. Decso moved to climb over the barricade to help her, but General Simon pulled him back. Simon was twice the size of Decso, and Decso didn't stand a chance against him. Decso was thrown back down the tunnel.

There was no other choice. She drew in a breath between blows and screamed. "Leandro! Massimo! *Help!*"

General Finn sneered and drew his arm back again. "Your screams are futile. No one can hear you."

Leandro leaped through the air at a Mad on Level Two. His teeth snagged the Mad's clothing and pulled it back to give his Pops room to snap its neck. Massimo was getting weak. Leandro knew that his dad needed blood if he was going to win a fight against Afana.

"Leandro! Massimo! *Help!*"

Leandro and Massimo looked at one another. They both heard Ryder screaming for help. Leandro wanted to go but didn't want to leave his Pops to fight the Mad on his own.

"Go, Leandro! *Go!*" Massimo yelled. "Ryder would only call for help if she really needed it."

Leandro bolted through the door and down the stairs. He had to take out the Mad as he went, which was slowing him down. There was no way he could leave them to go up to Massimo, not a chance in Hell.

He bounded down the stairs two and even three at a time. Leandro wanted to shout that he was coming and for Ryder to hold on, but he couldn't.

When Leandro got to Level Four, his friends were all there fighting against the Mad. They looked like they were winning. Why would Ryder call for help if they were winning?

"What're you doing just standing there, Fluffy?" Carter yelled as he pulled his axe out of the head of a Mad and hacked at the next. He had to work not to slip in the blood and guts carpeting the floor.

Next to a bloody body was a familiar spear. *Ryder?* Leandro's heart pounded hard with every step he took closer. The blood made it impossible to scent who was holding it. *Is it Ryder? Am I too late? Pops could have handled the Mad on the steps. He's a vampire, after all. I shouldn't have waited... I shouldn't have taken so long...*

He gingerly headed closer to the spear. Leandro's eyes trailed from the hand clasped loosely around the spear and up the arm. The arm was tanned and long and had blood splatters. He instantly knew that wasn't Ryder's arm. Hers was pale and lean. It was Koda.

Koda's finger twitched on the shaft, startling Leandro. He was alive? Leandro growled at Carter.

Carter realized what was happening and called the others over to protect Koda from the Mad.

Leandro raced off to find Ryder.

Carter watched Fluffy head back to the stairs. He knew that Fluffy wasn't scared of a fight, so where was he going?

Carter quickly followed Fluffy down the stairs.

"You fucking pussies," Ryder snarled at the generals between punches. She wasn't going to let them win. Every punch she took, Ryder made sure she was falling in the direction of the knife. If only she could reach it! But each time she got close, another punch would knock her in the other direction.

"Get off her!" Decso yelled. He was back at the front of

the tunnel and already climbing over the barricade. "You don't hit a woman!" He continued to yell as he forced his way over the barrier, slapping away the hands that tried to push him back. Ryder looked hard at each and every one of those faces. If she got out of this alive, they would pay!

Over the years, Decso had taken his fair share of beatings. Whenever Terrier or Ryder found it happening, they would stop the bully. Bullies always pick on the weak, which made Decso a perfect victim. He'd also never learned to shut his mouth. He always spoke before he thought.

Luckily for Ryder, today wasn't the case of Decso running his mouth too soon. He made it over the barricade and lunged for the knife on the floor by the dead Mad.

"Get him," General Finn snapped at the other generals. They headed straight for Decso, who paled. He'd actually thought that making a stand would stop them from beating Ryder. He realized that he hadn't really thought this out.

A man shouted from behind the barricade, "Don't touch Decso." It was Paul, who kept to himself normally. It looked like today was the turning point for some of the men. Today they had the chance to be their true selves.

The generals stopped at Paul's request. It wasn't because he was bigger than the generals. No, it was more because of what Paul represented—the hunters. The men the generals had kept down. There were more hunters than there were generals, and the hunters knew the generals didn't have any bullets in their guns—or Afana to back them up.

There was a tense standoff between the generals and

the hunters. No one moved, and General Finn even stopped punching Ryder.

He turned and looked at the hunters and his generals, then at Decso. "We won't hurt him," General Finn told Paul. Then he hit Ryder again, and only Decso objected. The men weren't going to help Ryder because she was a woman.

"Fuck you all!" Ryder spat through the blood and snot running down her face. "When I free this place you can all go die in the fucking woods with the Mad!"

Decso cringed.

"Not you, Decso," she managed as General Finn punched her again.

2 2

Leandro and Carter bounded down the stairs and landed on Level Five, "Those *fuckers*!" Carter was in full fury, and Leandro was feeling the same thing.

Man and wolf headed straight for General Finn. When the general saw Carter swinging his axe in his direction and Leandro's angry fangs, he instantly let go of Ryder and fired.

General Finn wasn't out of bullets, he had just been waiting for the right time to fire the gun. The bullet lodged in Leandro's thigh. Even beaten up, Ryder wasn't going to stand for that shit. No one shot at Fluffy.

The other generals had loosened their grips enough for Ryder to break free, and she took the chance and kicked General Finn right in the balls, then lunged and took him down to the ground. Ryder landed on top of him, driving the breath from his body. Ryder didn't waste her chance. She rained punches on General Finn, smashing the hell out of his already-battered face.

She heard Carter fighting with the other generals. They'd gone back to being useless without a leader, and they didn't know what to do with a wild man like Carter. She also heard Fluffy snarling and snapping, but he'd been shot in the thigh. A bullet wound wouldn't stop Leandro from growling at the generals, however.

General Finn fought back against Ryder, or at least he squirmed fruitlessly while she pounded him. She couldn't just punch him to death, though.

"Ryder, here." Decso was in front of her with the bloody knife.

General Finn's eyes bulged when he saw the blade. Now Ryder had the upper hand. She pressed the knife against his throat. "Tell them to stop," she ordered.

He spat blood at her. "Never."

Ryder pushed the blade harder against his throat. The skin parted, and a small rill of blood trickled down Finn's neck. "Tell them," she warned, "or I cut your fucking throat and watch you bleed out."

"Stop," he whispered.

Ryder pushed a touch harder. "Louder, asshole!"

He yelled through gritted teeth, "*Stop!*"

As Ryder had hoped, the generals stopped. It was like they were programmed to follow orders. Ryder wondered if Massimo could reprogram them to not be jerks.

A noise behind Ryder made her turn.

Terrier and General Murray had made their way onto the level where Ryder was, General Murray by Terrier's side.

Ryder thought that her head was screwing with her.

Her best friend and the man who'd put her in here together? *It can't be.* Ryder thought.

General Finn looked like he'd just shit himself, and rightfully so. Terrier was double the size of General Finn. He landed one punch on Finn's chin, and he was out cold. The other generals stepped away from Finn. They didn't want to be associated with him now.

General Murray went for the men around Ryder, and he didn't even need to touch them. The anger in his eyes said it all. The men backed away as one.

"Who else did this to you!" Terrier demanded as he glared around the level growling like Fluffy at all of the generals.

Ryder was overjoyed to see Terrier. "Come here, you big lump!" She grinned and held her arms out.

Terrier peered at Ryder, and a grin split his face nearly in two. His arms went straight around Ryder, and he had to remember not to squeeze his best friend too hard and injure her further. Ryder rested her head against Terrier's chest. She'd wanted to hug her best friend for years, but never could. Today she needed that hug more than ever. She let out the biggest sigh of her life. She'd made it.

Terrier examined her bruised face. "You came back."

"I said I would, didn't I? And I brought some friends with me." Ryder looked past Terrier toward the stairs. All of her friends were gathered there with their weapons ready to attack, although they were a bit late to the party.

Terrier looked at all the new faces and then back to the face he'd thought he'd never see again. "I've missed you," Ryder told him.

Terrier had a goofy grin on his face, "I missed you too."

Leandro let out a groan, and Ryder wiggled her way out of Terrier's hug to run to him.

Terrier held on to her. "Ryder what are you doing? It's a wolf!"

"It's Leandro. He's my friend."

Terrier looked at Ryder, confused. "It's a wild animal."

"He's not a wild animal, he's a werewolf, Terrier. I'll fill you in later, but he needs me now. Fucking Finn shot him."

"That jerk." Terrier kicked Finn for good measure.

Ryder ran to Leandro and dropped to her knees beside him. She stroked his fur on his thigh as she gently explored the wound. The bullet hadn't gone through. Ryder knew Leandro was a fast healer, but he couldn't heal while the bullet was in him.

"This is going to hurt," Ryder told Leandro as she stroked him. She really didn't want to cut out the bullet, but she knew that she had to. Ryder took a deep breath and slid the knife into Leandro's thigh muscle, and he whimpered in pain. She couldn't stop, but maybe there was a less painful way to get the bullet out than fishing around in Leandro's leg with a knife designed for fighting. She put the knife down and inserted her finger into the cut she'd made. Leandro whined, but she pushed ahead. She felt the bullet with the tips of her fingers, then maneuvered them under it and began to work it out. *Is this working?* Ryder began to panic. She was in too deep and there was blood everywhere, but the bullet was almost out. She had to continue. Ryder crooked her fingers and the bullet came out a little more, a little spurt of blood preceding it.

"Nearly there," Ryder told Leandro to reassure him.

Ryder gave one last tug and the bullet popped out

along, with more blood. "I need something to press on the wound," Ryder called. In the meantime, she pressed her hands against the open wound to staunch the bleeding.

Terrier ripped the nearest general's sleeve from the shoulder seam and passed it to Ryder.

Ryder took the sleeve and tied it around Leandro's thigh. She stroked his head, and he looked up at her. "You'll be all right." Ryder was happy that her friends were around her, but they needed to get out of here.

Leandro rubbed his muzzle on Ryder's chin. He was already feeling better. It was funny how Leandro could show affection when he was a wolf, yet when he'd been human he'd been shy and a little awkward—except for the dance she'd shared with him. Ryder ran her hand through his fur and got to her feet.

Ryder looked at the stairs, where there was a group of pole-wielding women. They looked more threatening than the Merry Men, who were looking more than a little scared. The women only had eyes for two groups of people, the generals and the hunters.

You could cut the tension with a knife. Carter was right in the middle of the two groups, so he gingerly stepped away from them and hid behind Ryder, "I'm with Ryder." He smiled at them to show he wasn't a threat.

The women looked at Ryder for confirmation. "He is. My friends are the good guys. They came to free you." She grinned, then winced at the pain. Her cheekbones had taken a lot of punches over the last few days.

Jasmine looked Ryder over. "I like your upgrade. Being a woman is a way better look on you." She pointed the metal pole at the generals and hunters. "What are we going to do with them?"

Ryder knew what she *wanted* to do with them, and also what the other woman wanted to do—make them pay for what they'd done. But that wasn't the way to move on from what they had suffered. Ryder had waited too long, though, and the women were already heading over to the generals with their poles, ready to attack.

"Stop!" Ryder yelled. "We can't turn into them."

Jasmine shook her head firmly. "Ryder, you didn't have to live down there on Six. You weren't used whenever one of these," she waved her pole at the assembled men, "wanted somewhere to bury their dick." Jasmine tilted her chin, and the other women agreed she was right. "They *need* to pay."

Ryder looked at the hunters and generals. While she was getting beaten, no one had come forward to help her except Decso. If they got out of the bunker they wouldn't help anyone, and the women would always be scared that one of the would capture them again.

"You're right," Ryder agreed.

The woman cheered, and the men shit themselves.

Ryder turned to the men like she was judge and jury. "Their punishment is to live on Level Six. They will never see daylight again."

The men shouted obscenities at Ryder, calling her every name they could think of. All of the men showed their true colors. Ryder didn't regret her decision not to kill them. A quick death would have been too easy for them anyway. They were finally getting served the punishment they deserved, and the women would get the Justice they deserved.

The women, on the other hand, were cheering Ryder's decision. "We need to get everyone off Level Six. Every section needs to be double-checked. We have to make sure not a single person is down there before we send the men down," Ryder explained.

"Um, Ryder? What about me?" Decso asked nervously, his finger raised.

Ryder smiled. "Except for Decso. He was the only one who did the right thing and helped me."

Decso let out a big sigh of relief. The women looked at him a little confused, they hadn't expected Decso, of all of the men, to help. It wasn't because Decso was a jerk, but rather because he wasn't brave. However, he'd chosen the right time to step up.

"Hey, Ryder, what about me?" another man wanted to know.

Ryder laughed. "You've got to be kidding me! As fucking *if*."

Other men called to Ryder, and she just ignored them. Instead, she turned to Terrier. "Where's Natalie? Mama Lou?" She couldn't see Peter either. She panicked. "Where are they?"

Under the blood, Ryder could see that Carter's face had gone white.

Terrier's smile put Ryder at ease. He looked at Jasmine. "Tell them it's safe."

Jasmine quickly passed the message down to Level Six.

Within a few moments, Peter arrived. He stood in the doorway with the look of a killer in his eyes. His face quickly softened as Samantha's little hand wrapped around his.

"Ryder's back!" Samantha yelled. There was a patter of boots on the stairs as the rest of the kids came running up. All the kids were as happy to see Ryder as she was to see them. The kids swarmed her, hugging her with excitement and relief.

"Samantha worked out how to open the door from watching Advisor George. She's one smart girl," Peter told them, which made Samantha blush.

Carter's eyes were locked on the stairway, waiting for Natalie to appear. He didn't know what to expect. She'd been the age of the kids when she'd been taken, but now she was a woman, and pregnant at that.

Carter's heart was out of control, bounding like a crazy drum. He pulled down on his beard and it was wet, then he looked at his hands, which were covered in blood. He couldn't have Natalie seeing him look like this.

He took a jacket from a general who was beside him and used it to wipe his face, then dropped the jacket on the floor.

A large dark-skinned lady appeared in the doorway, and Carter shot Ryder a look that said, 'That's not her. Are you blind?'

Ryder couldn't help but laugh, and she shook her head, "Mama Lou!" Ryder beamed, and a smaller person bobbed around Mama Lou. It was Natalie.

Carter's eyes were locked on her as Natalie looked at the new faces. She smiled when she spotted Ryder. She looked well, Ryder thought. Terrier headed over to Natalie, who looked like she was ready to have the baby any minute.

Carter quickly glanced at Ryder, and she nodded to confirm it was her. Ryder's emotions welled up inside of her; she'd been able to reunite brother and sister. Ryder wondered how many other people she'd be able to reunite. Many of these kids hadn't been born here.

Ryder stepped closer to Natalie and nudged Carter to follow her. "Natalie, someone would like to say hello." Terrier looked at her and then at Carter.

Natalie looked at Carter, confused, but her confusion started to fade. It had been twenty years since she had last seen Carter, and back then he didn't have a head of long hair and a face covered in a beard.

They stared into one another's eyes. The eyes never lied.

"Natalie?" Carter began nervously.

"Carter?" Natalie replied in the same tone.

The two of them froze, and everyone felt a little awkward that they were intruding on their special moment. Still, they couldn't stop watching since all of them were hoping for their own reunions soon enough.

Are my parents still alive? Ryder wondered.

Others were thinking similar things. My brother... My sister... Where are they now? Will they remember me? And the question everyone in the bunker had, "Why didn't they rescue me?"

Ryder wasn't going to get soppy now. She had come to rescue them, but they weren't out yet. Once they were, she'd go and find her family and be reunited like Natalie and Carter.

Carter stepped closer to Natalie, who raised her hand haltingly. "Can I?" she asked, and he nodded.

Natalie brushed his hair out of his face and went up on her tiptoes, then looked into his eyes, "Carter!" Her curious look changed to one of joy, and Carter's mirrored hers. "Carter...you're here! You're really here." Tears of joy flooded into Natalie's and Carter's eyes.

"Natalie! My little sister Natalie is all grown up." Carter was in shock at how his little sister looked, which was not so little anymore.

His arms were wrapped around his sister, the fingers just able to touch. Her overgrown belly was stopping them from fully connecting. He remembered how he used to be able to pick her up and swing her around when she was only six.

"We did this." Ryder beamed at Carter and Natalie, then at the Merry Men. "Brother and sister, finally reunited."

Natalie wriggled and looked at Terrier, who was standing near her. Terrier always kept a watchful eye on Natalie.

"Are you the baby's father?" Carter asked.

Oh, damn. Ryder really wished Carter hadn't asked that question. She could feel the tension from the hunters behind her, who were being guarded by the Merry Men. It could be any one of them.

"Yes," Natalie replied quickly, much to everyone's amazement. She smiled sweetly. "If he wants to be, that is."

A single tear rolled down Terrier's face.

Ryder kept her reaction in check so as to not ruin the moment. *I'll be damned! Finally, Terrier has a girlfriend. Only took me leaving the bunker, Mad on the loose, and Afana hunting him down for him to hook up. Nice!*

"I... I... I'd love to," Terrier mumbled and gently embraced Natalie. Carter stepped forward, ready to break them up, but then retreated. His sister was a grown woman, and Carter would have to come to terms with that.

"Terrier's one of the good guys, like you and Leandro," Ryder whispered into Carter's ear, then turned to check on Leandro. He was gone. "Shit! Shit! Shit! Massimo is still fighting Afana, and Leandro must have gone to help. We've got to help them." Ryder looked around in a panic. There was so much to do, and not enough Merry Men to do it all.

Murray had the solution. "We'll get the men down onto Level Six. You help your friends."

What kind of upside-down world have I come back to? Ryder thought. "*You'll* send the men down to Level Six?" Ryder snorted, although she hated it when she made that noise.

Carter laughed at her.

"Shut up, Carter. And you say *I* have bad timing." She rolled her eyes.

"Murray will help us," Terrier confirmed, backing the general up.

Ryder looked at Terrier in confusion. "General fucking Murray will help us? Did Finn really knock me over the head that hard? The head of the generals is going to help us?" Ryder was baffled.

Terrier started to speak, and Murray raised his hand to stop him. Ryder narrowed her eyes, and her hands landed on her hips.

Murray shuffled uncomfortably. "I'm not a general anymore. I haven't been since the second I had the opportunity to break free of Afana's control. I've done a lot of bad things in the bunker…a lot. I know whatever I do won't make it better, especially for you, Ryder. I won't ask you to forgive me."

Ryder cut him off. "I wouldn't."

Murray nodded as though her reaction was expected. "All I ask is that you let me help you now. Once everyone is free, you can do with me as you please. Any punishment would be justified."

She really must have taken a smack to the head. Was she hearing right? She could serve him the punishment he deserved? *What trick was he playing?*

Ryder feared that as soon her back was turned he'd double-cross them. "Why do you want to help us?"

"My son Martin is dead, so Afana no longer has a hold over me." He gulped back his emotion. This was the first time he'd spoken the words aloud. It made it all too real and painful.

Ryder knew Martin. He was one of the guards on Level Six, and he'd never caused any problems. Ryder liked to think that Martin would have been one of the good guys, given the opportunity. "I'm sorry for your loss, and I'm sorry it took you losing him to start making right your wrongs. Terrier, if he does one wrong thing, kill him. I've got to go."

Ryder bolted toward the stairs.

"We'll help as well." Jasmine slammed the pole into her hand; she really did like that motion. The women around her nodded.

Ryder knew that there was a lot of men on Level Five, and they were going to need all the hands they could get to make sure that there wasn't an uprising. After all, they were going to be sent down to Level Six, where they would spend the rest of their lives. Ryder wasn't planning on letting them starve. They had enough food down there to keep them going until they worked out how to let them into the tunnels with the crops. For now, they could stay on Level Six, and she'd let them think they were going to stay there. A nice shock to their system might turn them around, Ryder thought. Damn her bleeding heart. She dismissed that idea quickly. Those jerks hadn't helped her when they had a chance. Only Decso had.

Those fuckers could rot.

Vicky was at the foot of the stairs. "You up for some company?"

Ryder shrugged. "Sure."

"Good, cause I'm up for swinging my shovel at some more Mad."

"Count us in as well," Byrant and Graham chorused.

"And us," Maxwell added. Louis and Andrew nodded.

"I've only got a few bullets left, mind you," Graham told her. "I'll save them for when we need them most."

"Good idea," Ryder agreed.

"Ryder…" Willard muttered weakly. He'd taken a bad tumble when he fell down the stairs, and his ankle was all jacked up. It made Ryder wince. She was in pain but had no broken bones. "Tell Massimo he can keep his record player and records. Being here to help these guys is gift enough. Here, take these." He passed Ryder his knives.

"Thanks, Willard. That's kind of you. I'll tell Massimo, and I know he'll be happy. My friends will make sure you get up top safely," she said, then headed up the stairs.

Terrier looked at Carter. "Please watch over Ryder, not that she needs it. I just want to make sure Natalie gets out safely, being pregnant and all." Terrier looked at Natalie a little nervously.

"Sure." Carter patted Terrier on the shoulder. "Just don't let anything happen to her."

Carter leaned in and gave his little sister another hug. "See you up top, little sis." He pecked her on the cheek and headed up the stairs after Ryder. "Wait for me, smelly!"

23

———————

Murray watched as Ryder and the others headed up the stairs to rescue their friend from Afana. *Did I just send them to their deaths? Did the man Afana turned me into betray them? There is no way they will live in a fight. Two men and two women against him? They don't stand a chance in Hell. What have I done?*

Some of the women from Level Six had gone back down to their level to make sure all the women and children were out, along with the men who had fought alongside the women. Also to make sure that the Mad stayed down there. The other women kept a close eye on the generals and hunters who would shortly be moving into Level Six. Murray thought their punishment was fitting. He didn't care that his punishment was only that he do the right thing until his death.

Mama Lou, Peter, and Terrier had the situation under control, so they didn't need him, Ryder did. Murray headed toward the stairs.

"Where are you going?" Terrier asked. Everyone's eyes were on everyone's movements, so there was no way he was going to be able to sneak out. Also, that was no longer him, if he were honest.

Murray paused. "To help Ryder and the others. You've got this in hand."

"I'm going with you," Terrier told him.

Leandro ran up the stairs as quickly as he could. Ryder was safe now, and he needed to make sure Massimo was okay. His thigh was killing him. He'd never been shot before. His leg was already healing, which was another good thing about being a werewolf.

Luckily all the doors were open, because if they weren't, he'd be trapped. There was a downside to the doors being open—there were two Mad on the stairs.

The Mad's hands went for Leandro and he growled as he ran by, but it didn't stop them. The Mad were fast, and on a good day Leandro would be faster than them, but today wasn't a good day.

He needed to think on his paws and get the Mad before they could get him, since he knew he couldn't risk biting them and contracting the Madness. Leandro went for one Mad's legs and knocked it down, then leaped over it and bounded up the stairs.

Leandro had left Pops on Level Two. Leandro glanced over his shoulder and saw the Mad he'd leaped on stumble onto Level Three to search out its next meal, the other Mad following it.

Leandro wanted to go make sure there were no civilians on Level Three for the Mad to snack on, but if he did he'd have to leave his Pops for even longer with Afana. Leandro made his decision. He would save his Pops.

When he got to Level One, he could hear equipment crashing to the floor before he could see what was causing it.

Massimo and Afana were having one hell of a fight. Leandro sprinted over to his Pops. A scalpel flew toward Leandro and landed in his thigh. *Holy schnikes! Why is everyone attacking my thighs?*

Leandro turned to face the direction from which the scalpel had come and dragged the scalpel out of his thigh as the advisor threw more at him. Luckily for Leandro, none of the others hit the target.

Leandro ran at the advisor and knocked him to the floor, then leaped on top of him and sunk his teeth into the man's neck, stopping him from harming anyone else.

Leandro sprinted to Massimo, who was fighting Afana in the lab. The place looked like two Tasmanian devils had been in there. The lab was trashed; beds were flipped over, and other pieces of equipment were bent and scattered around the room.

Leandro jumped at Afana and sunk his teeth into Afana's flesh. The vampire's skin was tougher than a normal person, so Leandro couldn't get a grip, and Afana swung around and threw Leandro off him. He landed on his paws and went for Afana again, this time at his ankles. He pulled at Afana, unbalancing him.

Massimo used this weakness and swung at the other vampire, landing a punch on Afana's chin.

Afana spat blood. "Is that the best you've got?" He laughed at Massimo. "You should have stayed forgotten." Then Afana breathed in and out deeply. He was out of breath and appeared to be weaker than Massimo.

"Why couldn't Bethany Anne have found you and killed you before the WWDE?" Massimo replied.

"I would have killed her as well," Afana said happily.

Now it was Massimo's turn. "Don't make me laugh. A pissant like you couldn't have killed Bethany Anne."

Afana laughed. "She'd just be another addition to my cattle, a toy for me to experiment on." Afana looked at Knuckles, who thrashed around in his restraints, and Tank's headless body, which was on the floor after the vampires had slammed one another against the bed. "Now I have a new test subject. You!"

Afana quickly turned and sprinted out the door, and input the codes on the keypad. The door slid closed before Massimo and Leandro could get out.

Massimo pounded his fists against the door and Leandro clawed at it, but it made no difference; it was made from unbreakable glass. They had to get out of the room.

Advisor Robert came up alongside Afana from wherever he'd been hiding while the fight had been happening. "What would you like to do next?" Advisor Robert asked Afana.

Afana didn't answer. Instead, he stared at the wall. He wasn't looking at anything, which concerned Advisor Robert. He scanned his immortal leader and noticed rips in his clothing that revealed bite marks. Fear flooded through

Advisor Robert's veins at a frantic pace, just like the Madness in Afana's veins.

Advisor Robert stepped away from Afana. "Were you bitten?"

It took a moment for Afana to answer. "Yes, and I can feel the Madness inside me." He growled. "I need blood."

All this running up and down the stairs was way more exercise than she'd planned on doing and Ryder was knackered. The adrenaline kept her moving forward, and she wasn't going to let anything happen to Massimo or Leandro.

When they got to Level Four, where all the chaos had broken out, there were body parts all over the floor and blood coated everything it touched. Ryder saw a spear on the floor, and some of the Merry Men were helping Koda to his feet. He looked like he'd taken a beating, but he was alive.

Ryder wasn't going to let any more of the Merry Men end up like her and Koda. She needed to bring this fight to an end.

They moved up to Level Three, where they'd had another breakout of the Madness. Ryder couldn't leave the Mad alive since everyone from Level Six would need to move up through this level.

"Maxwell," Ryder started. But before she could finish, he did.

"We've got this level," he told her. Andrew and Louis

nodded, and the three of them entered Level Three to take on the last of the Mad.

Ryder and Carter made their way up the next flight of stairs, "I bet when we get to Level One, Massimo will have killed Afana and he'll be singing his favorite ABBA song. What was it again?" Carter asked.

"*Dancing Queen*," Ryder told him, remembering her dance with Leandro. She wondered if she remembered it so fondly because they wouldn't be dancing again.

Ryder lost her footing on the blood-soaked stairs and grabbed the handrail to keep herself from falling. Her heart had leaped into her mouth when she thought she was going to fall. Her almost-tumble had made a racket, and it echoed in the stairwell.

Carter quickly spun to her with his weapons drawn.

"It's okay, I just slipped. This damn blood is everywhere." Ryder grinned, a little embarrassed.

Carter rolled his eyes. "Watch your step."

"No shit, genius." Ryder laughed and took a moment to catch her breath. The others were at the top of the stairs, ready to enter the next level, and were listening to see if they could hear anyone on the other side of the door.

Hands grabbed Ryder's ankles, pulling her off the step. Ryder's hands clutched the handrail to stop her from falling. She looked down at a Mad with twisted legs on the stairs whose teeth were about to sink into Ryder's ankle.

Ryder panicked and tried to kick the Mad off her, but it was too late. Ryder felt the Mad's teeth bite down hard enough to break the flesh. Ryder thrashed to shake the Mad off. *I've been bitten... I've been* bitten! Ryder screamed inside.

Ryder was able to shake the Mad off, but it was too late, The Mad had Ryder's blood on her face. She wanted more, and she was pulling herself up after Ryder with her hands since her broken legs couldn't carry her. Ryder was in shock; she would become one of them soon. She was so close to being free she could almost smell it, and now what? The Mad had stolen her chance.

"Fuck you!" Ryder snapped. If she weren't going to be free, she'd make damn sure everyone else was before she turned.

Ryder went for the knives Willard had given her, wishing she'd picked up her spear since she could have staked the Mad before it bit her. Too late for regrets now.

She lunged at the Mad, but before she could connect with it, Murray was there. He pulled the Mad off the stairs by the legs and dragged her onto Level Four.

Murray returned, closing the door behind him. He wiped his hands down his pants, cleaning away the blood from the Mad he'd just killed; one of many.

"What are you doing here?" Ryder asked as she glared at him. Yes, he'd gotten rid of the Mad for her, but Ryder was just about to do it. He hadn't saved her life—although if he'd been here a few moments earlier, he would have.

"I thought you could do with some more help," Murray said, and he tried his hardest not to give her a look that said he was right.

"Why, because I'm a woman?" Ryder shot back.

Murray shook his head. "No, because Afana is an immortal vampire."

Good point, thought Ryder. They could do with help, but not from the man who'd led the other generals, and was

Afana's right-hand man when it came to stealing the innocent from their lives.

Blood started to flow from her bite wound, and Ryder pushed down her pant leg to ensure it was covered.

Murray eyed her warily. "You've been bitten?"

Ryder stared at Murray blankly. "Martin was bitten as well," he told her. "He went Mad within a few hours of the bite."

"Thanks for the update. I know what happens when you get bitten. Once I rescue everyone, they won't see me again," Ryder assured him. She was going to finish this, no matter what.

"Hey, are you all right?" Carter yelled down to Ryder.

"Yeah, just catching my breath. Looks like I should have gone into training before today," Ryder replied playfully.

Carter shouted, "Well, hurry up, slowpoke. There's a bit of noise on the other side."

Terrier came into view at the bottom of the stairs, fighting off the Mad.

"Don't say a word to them. I can't have them worrying about me. They need to focus on the job at hand,' Ryder whispered so only Murray could hear. "Do you hear me?" she ground out through gritted teeth.

Murray nodded. "I hear you."

"And kill me if I turn before I get away," Ryder added. She hoped that he of all people wouldn't have to, but he was actually the best person because then none of her friends would have to live with the guilt. If she made it out before turning, Ryder planned to take Bryant's gun and kill herself by the watering hole where she'd first had a taste of freedom.

Ryder played around with that idea. *Maybe not the best idea, since I'd have to cross the damn river again, which I would have died in if it wasn't for Fluffy. Then again, I am going there to die. But drowning?* Ryder's thoughts of where she was going to die made her chuckle a little, since there seemed to be no good place to die in peace.

"I will," General Murray promised soberly, as if he actually cared. He was a good actor.

Terrier had finished fighting the Mad and headed up the stairs toward Ryder. He looked at General Murray, then back at Ryder. "What's going on?"

They both shook their heads. "Nothing," Ryder told him. "I thought you were looking after the women and kids on Level Six?"

"Peter and Mama Lou have it under control."

Ryder replied quickly before Terrier could ask her any more questions, "It's nice to be fighting alongside you again. Come on, or Carter will be complaining."

Ryder quickly headed up the stairs to meet up with the others, Murray behind her. Carter glanced at Ryder. "Are you okay?" He looked concerned.

"I asked that." Terrier nodded at Ryder.

"Yeah, I'm fine, brought a friend with me." Ryder waved him on and smiled at Terrier. "What have we got going on behind the door?" Ryder asked to change the subject.

Carter explained, "There aren't any screams, so we're guessing there aren't any people left, or they are hiding, but there are grunts and groans, so we've got Mad."

"Let's take care of them quickly and get onto the Level Two." Ryder didn't know how long she had before she turned.

Everyone got their weapons ready, and Terrier cracked his knuckles. That beast of a man didn't need a weapon; he *was* the weapon. Ryder wished she had her spear. She checked that the knives Willard had given her were still in her waist belt, then got her bow ready.

Carter slowly opened the door, hoping that it wouldn't betray them and scream out to the Mad. Unfortunately, that was just what the hinges did. They creaked loudly, and the Mad turned to face them. Blood was dripping from the Mad's mouths; the generals had turned. Some were wearing their uniforms, others their civvies. The other Mad were the generals' wives and children. The only thing they all had in common was that they wanted fresh, juicy flesh.

The Mad ran at Ryder and the others, but they were ready. Ryder fired her arrows at the oncoming Mad, Graham swung his axes, and Vicky made the usual swings with her shovel. They were making quick work of the Mad, but these Mad were fast and strong.

Byrant fired his gun at the oncoming Mad until he was out of bullets.

Graham's axe lodged in a Mad's arm, and the Mad roared and kept trying to get Graham like it didn't have an axe buried in it. Graham pushed the Mad away from him using his axe, then swung the other axe into the Mad's head. His glowing red eyes were locked on Graham, and for a moment the Mad still went for him.

"This one won't die," Graham bitched breathlessly.

"It's 'cause you're not strong enough." Vicky laughed, mocking Graham as she swung her shovel at the back of the Mad's head. There was a crunch as she cracked his skull. "*That's* how you kill a Mad." She smiled smugly as the Mad dropped to the floor.

"True." Graham levered the axe out of the Mad. "Or like *this*." He ran to the next Mad, who was dressed in a uniform, and swung his axe. Aiming right for the neck, he used all of his force, and the Mad's head landed on the ground with a thud and bounced over to Vicky. The Mad's eyes were looking up at Vicky, his mouth was wide open, and there was blood dripping everywhere.

Vicky nodded. "That works too."

Terrier ran at a Mad in a berserker rage. He pushed his thumbs into the Mad's eyes, blinding it. The Mad flailed at Terrier, still wanting to taste fresh flesh, but Terrier wasn't going to let the Mad get a taste of *him*. He gripped the Mad's head and squeezed, using all his strength to crack the Mad's skull.

The gang made quick work of killing the Mad, but it was hard work, and the team were getting tired. They were nowhere near ready to give up, though.

"Get back up the next level of stairs," Ryder told them when they'd taken out the last of the Mad.

Everyone retrieved their weapons from the bodies of the Mad and headed up. Their weapons were covered in blood which was making it hard to keep their grip. Each of them wiped the blood down their pants, although it did little it did to improve their grip.

Ryder really wanted to take a shower back at Massimo's house and smell like lavender again.

This time Ryder made sure the door was closed behind them. She didn't want another sneak attack. Ryder couldn't believe she'd been stupid before and forgotten to close the door.

With every step, Ryder thought about when she'd change, or when they would face Afana. They were nearly at Level One, where he must be. She really hoped that

Carter was right and Massimo would be singing his favorite song.

Level Two was empty of Mad. Well, any *living* Mad. There were a few women and kids who didn't know what to do. When Ryder looked up at Level One, she could make out the giant monster that was Afana. She couldn't see Massimo or Leandro since most of the floor was covered in blood. *Was it their blood?* Ryder worried, and her heart stopped for a moment. This was it; time for her to face him.

"He's up there," Ryder announced, and the group wasted no time heading up the stairs to Level One.

"Now what?" Carter asked. He went for the door and stopped.

They didn't have a plan for rescuing Massimo and Leandro. "We rescue our friends. Give me a clear shot, and I will kill him." Ryder readied her bow and arrows. These arrowheads would break through Afana's tough skin. They had to.

"Sounds like a plan to me, stinky." Carter grinned. "Follow my lead. Ryder, you get in place for the shot, and a bit of notice would be nice. Last time she nearly took my ear off," He said to Vicky.

"You always exaggerate. It was nowhere near him." Ryder rolled her eyes, then nodded to Carter, and he followed orders and opened the door as quietly as he could.

This time the door didn't betray them. Murray did.

"Afana." General Murray shouted. Afana looked at Murray like he didn't know him. He was fighting the battle inside his body, the battle against the Madness.

Ryder's breath caught when Murray pushed her out of the way and headed straight for Afana. *The slimy double-crossing shitball. And I believed for even one moment that he'd changed. Fuck him,* Ryder thought.

If looks could kill, Terrier would be dead. Ryder had trusted Murray because of him. Terrier didn't see the look on Ryder's face because he started to go after Murray, but Carter stopped him.

Ryder pointed the arrow right at Murray's back as he walked over to Afana, but Carter pushed her arrow down. *What the fuck was he doing!* "Carter?"

"It's Tommy… Afana's got Tommy," Carter said, his voice full of fear.

Murray was blocking Ryder's view, and she leaned a little to see. First she saw Advisor Robert, then Afana, whose long fangs were protruding out of his gums, about to go into little Tommy's neck. Afana had Tommy in a tight grip, and he looked tiny next to the monster. Why hadn't the kid stayed put like Carter had told him? Why was he here?

Afana looked away from his meal at the quickly approaching Murray. "I've captured them for you, and Terrier is on Level Six," he announced.

I fucking knew it! Ryder's knuckles turned white as she gripped her arrows. They were worthless since Murray was blocking her target. *That yellow-bellied jerk.*

Afana looked as if he were grinning, but it was hard to tell since his face was like an uneven boulder. He stared at them for a long time without saying anything.

Advisor Robert looked at Afana, "Afana?" He waved, and it snapped Afana out of his trance.

Murray was beside Afana now and looking at Ryder and the gang. Afana still had a firm grip on Tommy, but Murray didn't even look at the poor kid. He was a monster like Afana, and Ryder had brought the whole gang to him. They'd followed his idea of splitting the group up, leaving them weaker.

With Murray now beside Afana, Ryder had a clear shot at both of them—but they had Tommy. Ryder knew that both men would use Tommy as their shield.

Advisor Robert stood alongside Afana as well, and it was clear that the wrinkly old fool was happy.

Carter, Vicky, and Byrant looked at Ryder with fear, since it was the first time they'd seen Afana up close. They didn't know what to do.

Ryder scanned the area for Massimo and Leandro. Where were they? They weren't on the floor. Ryder looked through the glass floor. Were they on another level, injured, and they hadn't seen them? Were they down one of the tunnels? Were they okay? The questions raced through Ryder's mind.

Ryder saw a flash of white behind Afana—Fluffy's tail. She shifted to peer behind Afana. Massimo was banging on a glass door, and Fluffy was scratching at the door next to him. They'd been trapped in another room. Massimo's clothes were ripped, there was blood on his face, and he was raging angry. His vampire fangs were out and he was ready to attack, but there was no one to sink his teeth into. It looked as though they'd had a fight and then Afana had locked them in the lab.

There were signs that Afana had been in a fight, but the blood could have been from the Mad he'd killed. At least

Ryder knew her friends were alive—and pissed off. If she could get them out of the room, they would stand more of a chance of getting out.

Ryder wished they had Samantha with them. She had been able to get the door to Level Six open, and maybe she could have done the same here.

"I was wrong about you, General Murray." Afana spoke in the deep voice that sent dread up the spines of everyone on the level.

Ryder felt almost physically ill. *He wasn't the only one wrong about* General *Murray.*

"You brought me the traitor and her friends." Afana stared greedily at Ryder. "Ryder, You were very good at hiding the fact that you were female. I knew there was something off after all of the years of watching you. I just wasn't sure what." Ryder was creeped the fuck out. She'd always known that she was being watched by a monster, but him actually saying it made it even worse.

Stop thinking about his bullshit and start thinking about how you're going to kill him, free the others, and ... Ryder stopped herself from thinking about what she'd do after that because there wasn't any point. The only point to her life was to rescue the others, and she would attempt that until she lost her mind to the Madness.

Afana grinned. "And you brought me Terrier, the traitor who was hiding on Level Six."

Ryder slipped the tip of the arrow into the alcohol and passed Carter the flint without Afana or the advisors noticing.

"Also, you brought me two more specimens to test." Afana stepped to the side, still holding Tommy in front of him to reveal Massimo and Fluffy. "I'm glad you did, since the other two didn't survive the testing."

General Murray must have brought Knuckles and Tank to Afana for him to run his tests on. Ryder remembered seeing Tank's body in the lab. He was mutated like Afana, and his head had been chopped off. Knuckles was apparently dead now too, and Afana had Massimo and Fluffy to run his new and awful tests on.

Ryder looked at General Murray. She didn't need to ask him if he'd brought Knuckles and Tank to the vampire, because from the look on his face she knew he had.

"I will deal with those once I've fed." Afana bent his head again and opened his mouth to sink his fangs into Tommy's neck.

"NO!" everyone yelled.

Ryder had seen what Afana had done to men when he drank their bodies dry of blood. Afana's drop hole was open. Ryder glanced down, but she couldn't make out if the other levels' doors were open. She had a feeling they were.

General Murray quickly leaned forward. "Afana, don't." He looked at Afana with something approaching panic.

Afana glared at him with glowing red eyes.

Murray shrugged. "He may be infected. I've never seen this kid. I think he's with them. He's an outsider."

"He is an outsider," Afana agreed. He looked at Tommy with disgust. "And I am already infected."

Everyone gasped. Afana was terrifying as a vampire monster. The thought of him turning Mad was unconceivable.

Afana looked at everyone with disgust. "Soon I won't be." He tightened his grip on Tommy.

General Murray gulped. He realized that once Afana's teeth sank into his neck, the boy would also have the Madness. "Has he been tested? Does he have the Madness?" General Murray asked Advisor Robert.

Advisor Robert shook his head, and General Murray looked at him like he was crazy. "Are you trying to infect our Immortal Leader?" General Murray barked.

Afana shot a killer look at Advisor Robert, and General Murray stepped closer to the vampire. "I was tested, and I'm clear of the Mad. All I ask is that you don't kill me." He tilted his head, revealing his neck for Afana to bite down on.

Everyone on the level was in shock. General Murray was offering himself to Afana to make him stronger and rid him of the Madness.

Afana knew that General Murray had the blood he needed, and he'd been waiting so long for him to come back. He wasn't sure he'd able to stop feeding on him and wasn't sure he wanted to. No one had ever made a request like this, but the general would be able to get the bunker back in order, and he wouldn't have to.

Afana edged forward, already tasting the liquid life flowing into his veins to make him stronger.

Afana released his grip on Tommy, and the lad ran over to Carter. Afana tried to stop him, but the boy was too quick. "I'll snack on him later," he growled. "And then the rest of you." Afana moved over to bite down on General Murray's neck.

Ryder slowly raised her arrow, since Afana only had eyes for General Murray. Afana's mouth was open wide, then he froze, and the sharp end of a blade was in his mouth.

Murray had stabbed Afana under the chin and pinned the vampire's tongue to the roof of his mouth. He pushed Afana away from him, revealing the handle on the blade under his chin. It was Willard's knife.

Murray had stolen one of the knives Willard had given Ryder. He must have taken it when he held Ryder back.

Ryder quickly raised the arrow, and she didn't need to ask Carter. He lit the flint. Ryder placed the end of the arrow over the flint, and her arrow was on fire.

Afana pulled the knife out of his mouth. It was covered in blood, and he was ready to kill Murray. He hadn't double-crossed them at all. Rather, he'd saved Tommy's life and given Ryder a clear shot.

Ryder let out her breath and let the arrow fly. Flames raged from the arrow as it headed straight for Afana. The arrow flew quicker than Afana could move, and it lodged over his heart.

Afana's eyes bulged as he worked out what had happened. He staggered backward, but he wasn't dead. The arrow had broken through his hard skin but had not pierced his heart.

Afana growled at them, and his arms windmilled as he lost his balance. Afana grabbed Murray as he staggered, and the general tried to get out of Afana's grip.

Ryder ran over to him, along with the others.

"I'm sorry. Please forgive me." Murray stopped fighting Afana. Instead, he grabbed the vampire in a bearhug and toppled them both into the drop hole.

Ryder watched as Afana's body thrashed as he tried to

grip the edges of the hole to halt his fall. Murray kept his hold on Afana and ensured that he couldn't catch the edge of a hole on the way down.

"I forgive you," Ryder yelled down to Murray.

Everyone else looked down silently as the two men plummeted down and crash-landed on Level Five with a thud. Screams of horror came from Level Five, since they hadn't been expecting them.

Murray's lifeless body lay on top of Afana's. The force of the impact with Afana's body had killed him instantly.

Ryder waited to see if there was any movement, but there was nothing. *They were free.*

Massimo... Leandro! Ryder stared at the keypad, but she didn't know the code.

"What's the code?" Ryder asked Advisor Robert.

"684532." Advisor Robert told her without any additional persuasion. He knew who was in charge now.

Ryder typed the code in, and the door unlocked.

Massimo and Fluffy walked through the door, "I nearly had him," Massimo complained, shaking his head in disappointment.

Ryder smiled. "We've got him now." She stroked Fluffy when he came to stand beside her.

They all looked down through the hole. The women from Level Six stood around the bodies.

Then Murray moved. *He'd survived the fall? How?* Murray's body was rolled to the side. He wasn't alive, Afana was. *Oh, shit!* They were all the way up on Level One, and he was on Level Five.

Ryder started for the stairs, but Carter stopped her. "They've got it. Look." Ryder looked back down the drop hole, and Carter was right. They *did* have it. The pole-welding women were beating the last bit of life out of Afana. It was their turn to get the revenge for the stolen years of their lives.

Ryder let out a sigh of relief when there was no more movement from Afana. He was dead.

She'd done it. No, Ryder thought as she looked around, *they'd* done it. Ryder and her friends had freed the women and children from the bunker.

They are free, and we are free. Am I *free?* Ryder thought for a moment. She might be free, but she wasn't okay. She'd been bitten by a Mad, and would soon turn. "Just need some fresh air. This place stinks of the Mad. Can you make sure they get out safely?" Ryder asked.

Everyone looked at Ryder, confused. Why wasn't she celebrating? her friends wondered.

Massimo looked Ryder up and down, and his eyes rested on her ankle and the blood stain. "Ryder, have you been bitten?"

Ryder nodded.

The color drained from her friends' faces.

Terrier shook his head. "You...you can't be. You just freed us." Terrier was in shock. He felt like he'd failed Ryder; like he'd failed his sister.

"I have been," Ryder told Terrier soberly.

She turned to her new friends. "Thank you for everything. In the last few days, I've lived more than ever before. Please, will you all look after my friends?" Ryder asked frankly.

"Of course. I'm sorry." Massimo shook his head sadly. If

he'd taken care of Afana sooner, she wouldn't have had to come up here and might not have been bitten.

Ryder looked at Massimo warmly. "Sorry? You've got to be kidding me. If it wasn't for your help, they wouldn't be free. You guys are my heroes!"

Massimo smiled. "You're the true hero." Massimo embraced Ryder, and Carter joined them. Fluffy rubbed his body against Ryder's legs, and she stroked his back.

"This isn't right." Massimo shook his head again. "I'm not letting it happen. Carter, your knife." Massimo held out his hand for Carter's knife.

Carter held out the knife for Massimo. "What are you going to do with it?' Carter asked as Massimo took the knife from him.

Terrier got between Massimo and Ryder, blocking the knife from being anywhere near Ryder.

"Terrier, he's a friend. Let him explain why he wants the knife." Ryder stepped around Terrier so she was in front of Massimo.

Massimo wiped the blade on his pants to remove all the blood, "I'm going to save Ryder's life. Well, my blood is going to…I hope." He slit his palm, and blood instantly oozed out of it. "Ryder, please show me your bite."

Ryder wasn't sure how Massimo's blood was going to help, but she'd try anything. She rolled up her pants to reveal her angry bite.

"Would you sit on the floor?"

Ryder did as he requested.

Massimo knelt beside Ryder and dripped his blood into the bite.

Everyone watched in wonder. "How is this going to work?" Ryder asked.

Massimo looked into Ryder's eyes, "I'm hoping that the nanocytes in my blood that make me a vampire will stop you from getting the Madness."

It made sense to Ryder. When they'd been walking to the bunker, Massimo had told Ryder that nanocytes were like little computers. *Maybe the little computers would work?* Ryder hoped so. "Do you think it will work?" she asked.

Massimo looked at her soberly. "I'm not sure," he admitted.

Ryder smiled at Massimo. "Thank you for trying." Ryder rolled down her pant leg, and Terrier helped her get to her feet. "I'm not going to risk being around you guys if it doesn't work," Ryder informed the group. "I'll come back if it does." She did her best to keep an optimistic tone.

Terrier's big arms wrapped around Ryder, embracing her. When Ryder rested her head on his chest his heart was beating frantically, yet Ryder felt quite calm. She was leaving the bunker a free woman. She let Terrier hold her longer than she wanted him to, since it was for him more than her. Finally, she stepped away from Terrier.

None of them knew what to say. Carter's eyes were starting to glaze over with tears, but Ryder couldn't have Carter crying since it would set her off. "Carter, don't forget to show Tightwad the toy box and see if he shits a rainbow." Ryder headed to the exit.

"See you later, smelly," Carter yelled to Ryder.

"Later, douchebag," Ryder yelled back.

25

The sun shone down brightly on Ryder's face. She inhaled the fresh air, and it did indeed smell a hundred percent better than the bunker. Ryder took in a deep breath and savored the sweet smell of freedom.

She'd done it. Everyone was free.

There was a patter of paws behind her. It was Fluffy. Ryder smiled as he bounded over to her. "What are you doing? I asked you to look after my friends," Ryder chided him.

Fluffy just looked up at her with his large orange eyes and rolled them.

Ryder grinned. "Stop rolling your eyes at me, Leandro!"

She was happy for the company, and Ryder knew that when she turned he'd stop her from hurting anyone.

A few women and kids were standing outside the bunker, and they all stared at Ryder like lost puppies. Ryder smiled at them warmly. Massimo would help them.

"What do we do now?" a woman asked Ryder.

"Live free," Ryder told her with a grin.

Ryder kept walking. Her job here was done. Leandro walked alongside Ryder as she entered the forest. She had her bow over her shoulder, and a quiver full of arrows. Ryder wasn't planning on using it, but she felt naked without it.

She strolled through the woods, stopping when she got to Graham's cart and the horses.

Ryder's face lit up. "Graham wouldn't mind if I borrowed Black Beauty one more time, would he?" Ryder asked Leandro.

"I'll take your silence as a no." Ryder grinned and ran her hand over Black Beauty's silky coat. The other horse would be able to pull the cart, so she wasn't going to leave the gang without a way to get the cart back to Pinewood.

Ryder unhitched Black Beauty and mounted the horse.

Ryder looked left and then right. She couldn't go left since that would lead her to Pinewood. There was no way she was going straight since that would mean crossing the river. *Right it is.* There were empty fields full of lush green grass. That would do. There'd be no one around for a long time.

"You ready for a run?" Ryder asked Fluffy. He chuffed at Ryder and sprinted ahead. "Cheater!" she called after him.

Ryder loosened the reins and nudged Black Beauty to make him go faster, and she was soon galloping beside the wolf. The wind whizzed past Ryder's face as she picked up speed. Her heart raced with every stride.

She was free!

The ride was her best, and her last ride ever. Ryder wanted to keep on riding, but she was concerned that if she rode too far, she might get to another area where there were people.

Ryder hopped off the horse and went to tie the reins to a tree, then stopped herself. The horse could be free as well.

She sat down on the grass and rested against a rock. Fluffy sat beside Ryder and placed his head on her lap. Ryder stroked Fluffy's fur. "Thank you, Leandro." She looked into his eyes. "I wish you could turn back to Leandro. I'd like to see you and hear your voice just one more time."

Ryder knew that wasn't going to happen. "Actually, don't bother. You can keep me warm instead." Ryder closed her eyes, wondering if she'd be Mad when she woke up.

Ryder pulled up her pant leg, and there were still teeth marks from the bite. She pulled her pant leg down to cover it with shaking hands. The adrenaline had left her body. Ryder was drained.

She let the tiredness of the day and the joy of saving her friends comfort her. Fluffy curled up beside her and they fell asleep.

Leandro watched Ryder through the night. He could see her eyes moving under her eyelids as she dreamed. He wondered what she was dreaming about, and hoped it was him. Leandro wished he'd had the confidence to tell her how he felt, or at least asked her for a date. Leandro laughed at that. He hadn't asked anyone out for a date for a year; not since he was at school, and even then he had been shy. He was the kid who liked to hide in the shadows to pretend he was invisible, and now he was.

He knew that by morning Ryder would turn into a Mad, so he drank in every element of her while she was still Ryder. Her skin was still silky smooth, with full lips he'd never kissed. He laughed inside at the thought of kissing her now with his wet snout. Ryder's cheekbones were perfectly defined, and her eyelashes were longer than the hair on her head, which had grown a little over the last few days.

He thought she was beautiful, but then he'd thought that from the first moment he saw her.

It wasn't only Ryder's beauty that had cast a spell over Leandro. It was…well, Ryder and her heart. She had been prepared to go back and save her friends at any cost. She would die for them. There lay the irony in it all. She had given her life for them to be free.

Live free or die, Ryder had once told Leandro,

How true those words were for Ryder.

Leandro laid back down next to Ryder, and her arm wrapped around his furry body once again. The fear of what morning would bring was hidden behind the peaceful comfort of each other's sleeping breath.

A gentle breeze danced over Ryder's skin, and she woke

with a start. Her body ached from the battles of yesterday —and the day before and the day before that—but she still felt like Ryder.

What the fuck? Murray had told her his son had turned a few hours later. It had been more than that—a lot more. The sun was at its highest point, which told her it was the middle of the next day. Ryder looked at her bite. It had gone to the bone, and still had dried blood around it. She had been bitten by a Mad, but wasn't Mad. How?

Ryder's throat was as dry as a cactus. *Ha, dry as a cactus.* She grinned, thinking about the jokes she'd made with Massimo about his cactus.

Leandro looked at Ryder. He was as confused as she was.

"Massimo's blood worked!" she screamed out loud. *"I'm immune to the Madness!"* Ryder actually leaped for joy. "I'm immune to the Madness!" Ryder yelled again. There was no one around to hear her happiness, so she ran over to Leandro and hugged him tightly, then paused. "Or is it just stalled? Like, the reaction takes more time for me?" Ryder played around with the idea. It was too early for her to make a decision. The one thing she knew was that she couldn't put anyone at risk. Ryder leaned back against the rock. Maybe she *would* be able to go back to Pinewood.

That thought warmed Ryder. She'd be able to see all of her friends again. She hoped Carter would be wearing Tightwad's colorful fairy-farted-on sweater, and that Massimo would be singing his favorite ABBA song at the top of his voice.

Ryder thought about the look on Carter's and Natalie's

faces when they were reunited. Ryder could have that as well.

If the Madness hadn't taken her, she could go *home*.

FINIS

Hayley here. Thank you for reading *Escaping Madness*, and also my *Author Notes*!

Escaping Madness is all about family and laughter. My last week has been filled with the same thing, since we were on vacation.

It's been a long time since my family and I got to just chill out and enjoy each other's time. We all have very full schedules, and because of this we live for our vacations—plus, we love to travel!

For the last few trips, we've let our daughter Callie age nine, decide where we went, and the trips have been awesome. This time she wanted to go to Cuba.

I'd just returned home from a work trip to China, had hardly any sleep for twenty-four-plus hours, and had a few Mike's Hard Lemonades, and agreed it would be an awesome trip.

The next morning, I woke up with a hangover (honestly

not because of the cocktails) and emails that the Cuba vacation was booked! It looked like we'd have to go now.

Cuba one of the greatest places we've ever visited. The buildings were breathtaking and in ruins, just as I imagine the end of the world.

We stayed in the most famous hotel in Cuba, although at the time I didn't know that it was, it was just the cheapest hotel, (I found out later it was on special detail! Looks like I'm even cheaper after a drink!)

Once we got to the hotel, I think my husband lost a few brain cells. He drank shampoo thinking it was mouthwash. He wore a kids swimming cap that looked like a fish and had the storekeeper and customers cracking up laughing. (I said we laughed a lot).

People rode in vintage cars. We rode in one which was over sixty-five years old and beautiful, and other people rode horses.

Callie and I took a trip around Havana in a horse and carriage. We went down the back streets and met the local people. Dogs and cats laid out in the sun or went shadow-hunting.

After the carriage ride we checked out the local artwork on the streets, I bought Callie a puppet, and we sat in the park playing with the puppet bring it to life.

People weren't on their phones; they were hanging out together. It felt like we'd gone back in time.

I loved it there, but what I loved more was spending quality time with my family. We could be happy anywhere as long as we're together.

Coming home from the trip made me think about our futures. If we don't take care of it, we'll end up in ruins like the buildings, but if we take care of each other, we'll be like the vintage cars—together for more years than we can remember. (It was our wedding anniversary on the last day, and neither of us could remember if we've been married for twelve or thirteen years! We've been together for over twenty, so we lost count.)

It made my dream of being a full-time author even stronger, and every new book helps our family come closer to our dream—spending more time together.

I'd like to thank Michael for helping me make our dream become our reality.

I'm off now to work on book four, and hang out with my family,

Hayley Lawson

If you loved, *Live Free or Die series* try out, <u>Contamination</u> (Invasion Survivor Book 1)

Humanity has one option.

Evacuate Earth.

After a wave of fear crashes over the world in response to a deadly virus. Fear intensifies when it's discovered that the virus is the first wave of attack by an alien race that wants Earth for themselves.

It's one day before Paige's eighteenth birthday, and the world is turning into the walking dead! Zombie-like people are seeking her out.

What the hell! Just Paige's luck.

Can Paige rescue her family and get off the planet before The Wave captures her?

Other books by Hayley Lawson

They Are Zillion here: https://www.amazon.com/Zapa-colypse-They-Are-Zillions-Book-ebook/dp/B07CV373R6/

The horde moves, thinks, and learns as one.

But Hunter doesn't know this. He just knows that they are sick, he doesn't want to kill sick people.

He's not a murderer, he's just a sheriff.

The infected move together, destroying everything in their path.

The doc said they can't see, maybe that's why they keep tearing down buildings.

But Hunter doesn't have time to figure that out. He promised his wife he'd get the kids, then save her.

First, he has to save himself- and try not to kill anyone in the process.

Book two: *Zurrounded* (They Are Zillions Book 2) - https://www.amazon.com/Zurrounded-They-Are-Zillions-Book-ebook/dp/B07DBWBFPF

Stay up to date with Zillions in the Facebook group:

https://www.facebook.com/groups/832626480256677/

First, THANK YOU for not only reading this story, but also reading through the back to our *Author Notes*, too!

When Hayley and I started working together, it was a clash of loves.

I loved a good adventure story where the main hero is working hard to destroy the bad guys and Hayley liked to kill everyone.

I mean, *EVERYONE*.

So, a year later I've got her seeing a bigger picture, but I had a conversation with her earlier where I realize that she still loves the killing.

Case in point. We have either weekly or bi-weekly updates on our projects (we have quite a few) and since it had been a while, I asked if it was one week or two since we talked last. I was thinking two, but wanted to make sure I just didn't lose track of days.

She explained it was two, that her family had gone on vacation to Cuba this last week.

"Cuba?" I wondered.

"Yes, it was awesome! One of the prettiest places I've been to I think, and I've been to many." She goes on to explain the juxtaposition between new buildings, and others that are still lived in, but are crumbling.

This made me think of Madness, our zombie story that isn't zombies (but totally is) and Cuba.

"You have GOT to see this movie, *Juan of the Dead*," I explain to her. "It's a zombie movie based in Cuba, subtitled."

Her face is giddy with excitement and she calls to her young daughter mini-Hayley to explain there is a zombie movie based in Cuba…

Now, they are *both* practically giddy with joy.

I'm shaking my head, thinking I'll never be excited like this to watch *any* zombie movie.

It is a comedy (I saw it in subtitles and enjoyed it). If you like comedy and like zombies (which you probably do, given that you're reading this book) I recommend the story.

I realized that the desire to kill everyone never left Hayley, it just went underground for a while.

Ad Aeternitatem,
Michael